"We all make mistakes."

"I'll bet you don't."

Lily's guileless brown eyes met his. Carter wanted to be as good as she believed he was. She'd shared her past so freely, hiding nothing.

"Oh, I've made my share of mistakes," he said.

As he eased the Lexus into a parking space, he considered sharing his, telling her about the daughter he didn't know. Except he couldn't work up a way to explain, not without stirring up questions he couldn't answer. No, the past was best kept that way—dead and buried.

"Nothing like mine, I'll bet," she said. "From now on I'm going to be more careful about who I get involved with. If a man isn't honest, I'm not interested."

Dear Reader,

This is the third book in the Halo Island miniseries. Everyone has secrets in their past, things they don't share. CPA Carter Boyle is no different. His secret is a painful one, dating back to high school. When his girlfriend got pregnant, Carter had big plans to settle down with her and their baby. But the girl ran away, taking Carter's infant daughter with her. After years of fruitless searching, Carter gave up and moved to Halo Island.

Lily Gleason is being audited. She needs help, and Carter is her man. Having come from a home filled with mistrust and lies, Lily values honesty above all else. From the moment she meets Carter, she can tell that he is an honest man. The kind of man she could fall in love with.

Then again, she doesn't know about Carter's secret!

As always, I welcome your e-mails and letters. E-mail me at ann@annroth.net, or write to me at Ann Roth, P.O. Box 25003, Seattle, WA 98165-1903. Also, please visit my Web site at www.annroth.net and enter the monthly contest to win a free book. You'll also find my latest writing news and a new, delicious recipe posted every month.

Happy reading!

Until next time,

*Ann Roth*

# Ooh, Baby!

## ANN ROTH

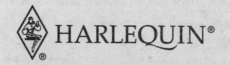

HARLEQUIN®

TORONTO • NEW YORK • LONDON
AMSTERDAM • PARIS • SYDNEY • HAMBURG
STOCKHOLM • ATHENS • TOKYO • MILAN • MADRID
PRAGUE • WARSAW • BUDAPEST • AUCKLAND

Special thanks to Dave Dierst,
the best CPA in Seattle. Thanks for answering my
questions about small business audits.
Any mistakes or misinformation are entirely my fault.

Recycling programs
for this product may
not exist in your area.

ISBN-13: 978-0-373-75256-0
ISBN-10:    0-373-75256-3

OOH, BABY!

www.eHarlequin.com

**Printed in U.S.A.**

## ABOUT THE AUTHOR

Ann Roth lives in the greater Seattle area with her husband. After earning an MBA she worked as a banker and corporate trainer. She gave up the corporate life to write, and if they awarded PhDs in writing happily-ever-after stories, she'd surely have one.

Ann loves to hear from readers. You can write her at P.O. Box 25003, Seattle, WA 98165-1903 or e-mail her at ann@annroth.net.

## Books by Ann Roth

### HARLEQUIN AMERICAN ROMANCE

Don't miss any of our special offers. Write to us at the following address for information on our newest releases.

Harlequin Reader Service
U.S.: 3010 Walden Ave., P.O. Box 1325, Buffalo, NY 14269
Canadian: P.O. Box 609, Fort Erie, Ont. L2A 5X3

## HENRI BOYLE'S SNICKERDOODLES

Makes 5 dozen

Combine:
*1 cup soft butter*
*1 1/2 cups sugar*
*2 eggs*

Stir in:
*2 3/4 cups sifted flour*
*2 tsp cream of tartar*
*1 tsp baking soda*
*1/2 tsp salt*

Chill dough for 30 minutes to one hour. Roll into balls the size of small walnuts. Roll in mixture of 2 tbsp sugar and 2 tsp cinnamon. Place 2 inches apart on ungreased baking sheet. Bake at 400°F for 8 to 10 minutes.

# Chapter One

"Hi, Lily, it's Janice."

As if Lily didn't recognize her sister's voice. "It's your mommy, Hailey—at last," she told the gurgling baby on her hip.

"Embla," Hailey said, her little lips blowing bubbles.

At seven months she wasn't old enough to make any sense, but Lily thought she understood. "Hailey says hello, and that she's excited to hear your voice." Moving into the living room, phone clutched in her free hand, Lily squeezed between the armchair and the compact desk that served as her office. "You know I adore Hailey, but I'm leaving soon for that lunch with my friends. For my, ahem, birthday?"

"Omigosh, it's April thirtieth, isn't it? It completely slipped my mind. Thirty on the thirtieth. Happy birthday, Lily. Or should I say, old lady."

Lily winced. "Very funny. Well, you're not far behind."

Hailey was heavy, and after stepping over the baby-paraphernalia-laden coffee table, Lily sank onto the love seat. She propped the baby close beside her, keeping her arm around the little body. "In just two short years *you'll* be thirty."

"I'd rather not think about that now."

While Lily completely understood, the response was typical Janice. At times her sister was as irresponsible as a teenager. "Back to Hailey. You were supposed to be here by now. You didn't forget that, too, did you?" Lily gave a forced laugh. "As if you'd forget your own daughter."

But that was a distinct possibility, since like their mother, when Janice fell in love she tended to forget everything but her man. At the moment she was dating a bass guitar player, and after bringing Hailey from Seattle to Halo Island so Lily could watch her, Janice had rushed back to the Seattle airport and caught a flight to San Francisco for a romantic weekend. She'd returned to Seattle this morning.

When Janice remained silent, Lily went on. "Your plane was on time—I checked. You were supposed to be here by now."

"I know, but…"

That little hesitation set off warning bells in Lily's mind. Hailey was squirming, so she laid her on her back. The baby waved her chubby little arms and legs in the air and rewarded Lily with a toothless grin.

"Did you miss the ferry?" The only way to reach Halo Island was via seaplane or ferry, and the ferry was cheaper.

"Not exactly. Oh, Lily, you'll never guess. Bobby invited me to tour with his band, all the way across the country! They might even let me sing backup! This could be my big break, and I'm just thrilled!"

Every statement was a joyous exclamation. As pleased as Lily was for her sister, who had forever dreamed of making a living as a singer, she wondered about Hailey. "Great, but do you think all that traveling is good for a baby? Remember how chaotic our childhood was, and how we always swore we wouldn't do that to our kids?" Not that Janice had ever wanted children. But then Hailey had come along. The baby's father was long gone.

"How could I forget something that important?"

Lily grabbed a rattle from the coffee table and handed it to her niece. Over the phone she distinctly heard an airport announcement. "You're in the Seattle airport," she guessed. The realization irritated her—why hadn't Janice just said so? She never stated the plain truth unless it suited her, another despicable trait inherited from their mother. "You should've told me sooner, so I could change my lunch plans." Too late for that now.

"Actually, I'm at LAX with Bobby and the band. Listen, will you keep an eye on Hailey while I'm gone?"

*LAX?* "But I—" Lily began, stopping when the baby exchanged the rattle for a hank of her hair—*shouldn't have bent down*—and pulled it toward her mouth. Lily gently untangled the strands from the pudgy fingers, then swiped a trail of drool off the baby's dimpled chin. "You know tourist season starts in two weeks. I'm swamped trying to make enough jewelry for opening day."

"You're always swamped. This'd only be for two weeks—three, tops."

Babies were all-consuming. Having just spent two and a half days with her niece, Lily understood this oh, so well. "You know I dearly love Hailey," she said, planting a quick kiss on the baby's foot. "But you also know how small this houseboat is. Six hundred square feet is barely room for me, and with my jewelry stuff everywhere…" She glanced toward the kitchen, where the small eating bar and two stools were piled with boxes of beads, fasteners, coils of metal wire, pliers and other supplies. Lily shuddered to think what would happen should Hailey get hold of any of it.

"Come on, Lily," Janice prodded. "You've always loved kids. Heck, you practically raised me. You're great with Hailey—much better than I am. She adores you."

Trust Janice to know exactly what to say. Lily *was* good with kids, and hoped to have a whole brood someday. She wanted what she and Janice had never had, a big, happy, stable family. With a loving husband at her side, a man who actually wanted his children, and neither of them lying to their kids about anything, ever. Yes, Lily had been burned by Jerome, who had wormed his way into her heart and bed before she found out he was married. Yes, that had hurt. But it had been over a year now, and she was ready to move on. At the same time, what with saving up to buy Mr. Creech's building on Main Street—he'd offered her a great deal, provided she came up with the down payment by fall—and steadily growing her jewelry business, there wasn't much time for dating, let alone babies. Yet her biological clock had begun to tick. Loudly.

"Lily? You there?"

"Listen here, Janice. Even if you forget about my lack of space, the hazards to Hailey's safety and the fact that I'm about to start putting in twelve-hour days, seven days a week, I'm really not ready for this kind of responsibility. Not even for a few weeks."

"And I so get that. But this is my big chance, and you just said that all the traveling wouldn't be good for Hailey. I don't exactly have anyone else to turn to. Would *you* leave a baby with our mother?"

Who at the moment was so wrapped up in her current lover, she barely stayed in touch. "No," Lily replied without hesitation. She released a heavy sigh. "All right, I'll do it. But you *have* to pick up Hailey before tourist season starts— no later than May fourteenth." A Sunday. With the season officially opening May seventeenth, that seemed reasonable.

"Thanks, Lily. I really appreciate this. I'll be in touch, or if you need to reach me, call my cell."

As the phone clicked in Lily's ear, Hailey stuck her toes in her mouth and gurgled.

SEATED AT A TABLE for four plus a high chair in the Salty Dog, a restaurant favorite of locals and tourists, Lily shared the latest from her sister while Hailey gummed a roll. "So I'll be taking care of my niece for the next two weeks."

Joyce and Cindy, Lily's two employees and also her friends, had already cooed over the apple-cheeked baby, who had charmed them with her big, blue eyes and rosebud mouth. Now they said nothing.

But Charity, Lily's best friend, spoke right up. "That's some sister you have. And with tourist season about to start. I'd like to give her a piece of my mind. Saddling you with—"

"Shh." Lily laid a warning finger over her lips and turned her gaze to the baby. "Not in front of Hailey. We'll talk later. It isn't every day a girl's friends treat her to lunch, and I want to enjoy every second."

"Personally, I'm glad you're doing this for your sister," Joyce said. "It isn't easy raising a baby alone." A divorced, thirty-three-year-old mom, she ought to know. She smiled. "That's why I'm eternally indebted to you for hiring me. Where else could I earn a decent income working out of my home?" Making the jewelry Lily designed. "It's so nice that I can do something for you by treating you to lunch."

"I second that," said Cindy, who was thirty-seven. Her husband, a ferry captain, had been injured in a freak accident and was on permanent disability, which didn't pay enough to support a family of four. He helped as much as he could with their two grade-school children, cooking meals and driving them to and from school. Cindy took care of the house and yard, and also worked for Lily, both from home and at the booth where Lily sold her jewelry during the four months it was open.

"It's Lily's big day, and we're all glad for the excuse to meet for lunch." Charity grinned at Lily. "You're gonna love this new decade of your life," she said, sounding as if she knew firsthand. And she was barely thirty-one.

Joyce and Cindy nodded.

"I intend to do my best." Lily straightened Hailey's bib, then picked up the menu and studied it. "The grilled crab and cheese looks good. That's what I'll have."

"I think I'll order that, too." Joyce closed her own menu. "I still have Kayla's stroller, if you want to borrow it. And a ton of baby toys and clothes."

"I could use a stroller, and since Janice only packed four outfits and a handful of toys, I'll take it all. Thanks."

While Wanda, the pink-uniformed waitress who had worked at the Salty Dog forever, took their orders and Hailey turned what was left of her roll to pulp, Lily glanced out the window. Dark clouds hung in the sky and pelted out a furious rain—not unusual for the end of April in the Pacific Northwest.

Before their food arrived, Lily opened the birthday cards from her friends. They were sweet and funny, and she laughed and passed them around. Hailey crowed happily— she adored people—and the mood turned festive.

In no time, Wanda arrived with their mouthwatering food and a fresh roll for Hailey. "You sure are a cutie-pie," she cooed, earning a delighted squeal from the baby. "You girls enjoy."

For a few moments Lily and her friends went silent except for murmurs of pleasure while they ate, with pauses to pay attention to Hailey, who entertained them with her babbling and bemused facial expressions.

At last coming up for air, Charity spoke. "Tourist season is grueling for all of us." Like Lily, she had her own business—wind socks and chimes—and rented a booth near the waterfront. They'd met there. "With Hailey to look after, how will you get ready?"

There was the twenty-four-carat question. "Janice promised to pick her up before the season actually starts, so that's something," Lily said, thinking positive. "I guess I need to find a sitter. Any ideas?"

"Not at the moment," Joyce said.

Cindy shook her head. "Me either, but I'll keep my eyes and ears open."

Charity looked blank.

Suddenly, bearing a cake ablaze with candles, a grinning Wanda made her way toward them. Everyone in the restaurant—this time of year, all locals—broke into song. "Happy birthday to you…"

Lily wanted to cry. She'd lived on the island only seven years, but the people were so warm and accepting, she felt as if she'd been here her whole life. When the song ended she swiped at her eyes. "Thank you all so much."

"Aw, you're welcome." After giving her a fond smile, Charity turned her attention to the cake. "Now, make a wish and blow out all those candles before they melt the icing."

"Aren't you the comedian." Lily didn't think long about what she wanted. With her jewelry business growing, the best friends ever, a cozy little houseboat and an old but reliable car, both paid for, her life was just about perfect. There was only one thing missing—a man to share it with.

Now that she was over Jerome, even if she was busy getting ready for tourist season, she ought to at least start looking for an honest, trustworthy man who liked children. Closing her eyes, she silently made her wish. *Please let me find my Mr. Right.*

She opened her eyes and blew with all her might, extinguishing all thirty candles plus the one to grow on. Everyone in the room cheered before the diners returned to their meals and Wanda headed for another table.

Lily cut the cake and passed out the plates. She placed a pink rose made of icing on the tray of Hailey's high chair. The baby stuck her fingers in it, then sucked them with gusto.

"I'll bet I know what you wished for," Charity said. "The money to buy that building on Main Street. I would kill for a prime location like that."

Every artist Lily knew was green over the bargain price Mr. Creech had offered her, and she grinned. "I'm sure that if the man lived in your neighborhood instead of mine, you'd have shopped for him and brought him meals after his knee surgery. Then *you'd* be the one saving up for the down payment. But I'm not about to waste a wish on that, since I've already saved most of the money. If this year's season is as good as the past few, I'll have the rest of what I need in plenty of time."

"Then what *did* you wish for?" Charity asked.

Cindy shook her finger. "If she tells, won't that cancel the wish?"

"Of course not." Joyce leaned in and lowered her voice. "Tell us, Lily."

Seeing no reason not to—they already knew she was ready to date again—Lily shared. "I'm not getting any younger and I want kids, so…I wished for a good man."

"I've been trying to find one of those since my divorce," Joyce muttered. "Lots of luck."

"When it comes to men, none of us has had much of that." Propping her chin in her hand, Charity sighed. "I wouldn't mind getting married and having a baby myself. But at the moment I'd settle for a decent date."

During the moments of heavy silence that followed, Lily wondered how she'd meet someone on Halo Island, which wasn't exactly teeming with single males. For a moment her spirits plummeted. But this was her birthday, and she wasn't about to ruin it with depressing thoughts. She smiled brightly. "Isn't this the best cake you ever ate?"

"It tastes homemade," Charity said, licking her fork. "So, birthday girl, what's on your agenda the rest of the day?"

"We need to stockpile more inventory so I'd planned on making jewelry. But now…" She glanced at Hailey. "Maybe during her nap."

"I'm happy to work more hours if you want," Cindy said. "Max needs a uniform for Little League, and we could use the extra cash."

Joyce nodded. "I can always use more money."

They were dependable, loyal, fast and good at the craft, and Lily needed them as much as they did her. Plus she loved them dearly. "You two are godsends. Go ahead and work as much as you want."

Hailey smeared her hair with her sticky hands, then began to fuss, signs that she was tired. "She needs a nap,"

Lily said, already anticipating a few hours of work time. "I'd better take her home. Remember, if you hear of a dependable babysitter, let me know. I'm willing to pay well."

Later, while the baby slept in the portable crib Janice had brought and squeezed into Lily's bedroom, Lily checked the day's mail before getting to work. No birthday card from her mother, but that was no surprise. Eventually she'd remember. There were four thick catalogs from the jewelry supply companies, the latest *O Magazine* and a thin, business-size envelope.

IRS, the return address said. Lily had paid both her annual and quarterly taxes. What could the IRS want from her? Drawing a blank, she opened the envelope. She read the letter and felt sick. They wanted money, lots of money, and were going to audit her. In mid-June, at the height of tourist season.

She massaged her temples, where a headache was starting. "Happy birthday to me."

IT HAD BEEN ONE HELL of a tax season, and thank God it was April thirtieth and almost over. Rolling his weary shoulders, Carter Boyle handed his last individual client of the season, Pete Downs, his tax return. "Since you're filing late, you'll be paying a penalty."

"I know I should've gotten it together earlier," Pete said. "But with the divorce and all…" He spread his hands in a helpless gesture. "At least it's done. Thanks for taking care of it so quickly."

"No problem, but next year, come in earlier. Be sure to ask my secretary, Linda, to send you a reminder."

As Carter walked his client to the door he thought about the months ahead, filled mostly with appointments with business clients. Those meetings took more time and the accounting was more complicated, but the pace was less hectic. Regular hours, weekends off and a few weeks' vacation in August—man, did he look forward to fishing and golf. And dating.

It had been a while, and he was more than ready for female company—in every sense of the word. A healthy, thirty-four-year-old male could go only so long without sex.

Standing on the threshold, he shook Pete's hand. "Take care."

"I will." Pete glanced around the office. "You have it all. A successful business, any woman you want. Wish I'd stayed single. This divorce has just about killed me."

Which appeared to be true. Since Pete and his wife had split, he'd lost too much weight and aged a decade.

"Actually, I've been thinking about getting married," Carter said. All his friends were happily hitched, and he was tired of playing the dating game. He wanted to settle down and start a family. One where the woman stuck around and he actually got to know his own kid… Now all he had to do was meet the right woman.

"You? Wow, I didn't know. Best of luck." Pete scratched the back of his neck. "Who is she?"

Carter had no idea. But that sounded crazy, so he smiled. "I'm not saying."

"Haven't asked her yet, huh? Guess I'll hear about that when it happens.".

In a town the size of Halo Island there was no doubt of that. After closing the door, Carter returned to his desk. He glanced over the file of his three-thirty appointment with D. J. Hatcher, a client who'd become a friend. D.J. co-owned Island Air with his employees, and Carter enjoyed preparing the company's quarterly returns. Yet after a moment his mind wandered to a place he preferred to avoid. To thoughts of his daughter. Lately she'd been on his mind a lot, probably because today was her seventeenth birthday.

*Happy birthday,* he thought, his heart empty and bitter. He didn't even know her name, and had no idea where she was. It wasn't that he hadn't tried to find her. God knew, both he and his parents had spent countless dollars and hours looking. A decade ago they'd stopped, after the unexpected death of Carter's father. A fatal heart attack Carter and his mom blamed on the relentless stress of their fruitless search. Having vacationed in the San Juan islands, and loving the beautiful setting and friendly community, his devastated mother had left Seattle for Halo Island to start fresh. Carter had waited until he'd finished grad school and done his time with a Big Four firm in Seattle. Then he'd followed her and opened his own accounting business.

After all this time, they both knew they weren't likely to find his daughter. No one on the island knew about her, and neither he nor his mother mentioned her anymore. It was too painful. But Carter figured his mom was thinking about her granddaughter today, and feeling just as low as he was.

Jaw set—he would not revisit his sorry past again—he pulled out his BlackBerry. He called up and paged through the address book containing the names and numbers of women he'd dated and liked well enough to take out again from time to time, provided they hadn't gotten married or moved away. Now that he was ready to commit, he considered each woman with a different eye.

Miriam Adams was cute and fun, but aside from a mutual physical attraction they shared nothing in common.

Sarah Baker had a little problem with promiscuity. Carter scrolled slowly through the rest of the list, but couldn't imagine spending a lifetime with any of these females. Best start fresh and—

His intercom buzzed, interrupting his thoughts. "Heather Larkspur is on the phone," Linda said.

One of the women in his book. They'd dated on and off, but not for a good year. Carter had bypassed her name, but now… Talk about good timing.

"Put her through." An instant later he greeted her. "Hello, Heather."

"Hi, Carter. It's been a while."

Her voice was smooth and melodic. She had a great body and was terrific in bed. Plus, she was easy to talk to. Carter thought he could trust her, too. He should've been salivating, but he felt nothing.

What was his problem?

Maybe he needed a physical. Or a psychiatrist.

"I was just thinking about you," he said. Which, since he *had* glanced at her name, was true.

"Then I'm glad I called. I'd love to go to dinner and catch up. Are you free some night this week?"

The least he could do was have dinner with her. Couldn't hurt, and maybe seeing her face-to-face would jump-start his interest.

"How about Thursday—my treat," he said, feeling optimistic. "What time should I pick you up?"

THE DAY AFTER her birthday, with Hailey asleep for the night, Lily sat on the love seat with the materials for a necklace. She ought to make a dozen tonight, but wasn't sure she had the energy. Between Hailey and squeezing in work whenever possible, she was exhausted. She longed to go to bed early, but there was too much to do—and to worry about.

The letter from the IRS had weighed heavily on her since she'd opened it yesterday. According to them, she owed a staggering amount of money in unpaid taxes, including penalties and interest. Enough to shut down her business and put her on the street.

The very idea tied her stomach in knots. Lose her home and the jewelry business she'd worked so hard to build? Let down Joyce and Cindy, and allow Mr. Creech's building to slip through her hands? It was all unthinkable and terribly frightening. Suddenly her fingers were too shaky for work. She set the necklace aside.

She needed help. Ryan Chase, owner of Halo Island Bank, was smart about money matters. He'd know what to do. Having only met him once, Lily didn't feel right about calling him at home. She knew his wife, Tina, better. They'd met a year ago, at the community center's monthly bunco game.

Tina's number was on the bunco players' roster provided by the community center.

"Hello, Tina, it's Lily Gleason," Lily said when Tina answered.

"Well, hello." Tina sounded both pleased and surprised, and no wonder. Lily had never called her.

"Are you going to bunco Saturday night?"

"Ryan's playing poker and Maggie's spending the night at G.G.'s, so yes." Maggie was Ryan's daughter, adopted by Tina when they married. G.G. was the retired kindergarten teacher who had raised Tina after the unexpected death of her father, as her own. "Are you?"

"If I can find a sitter." Lily explained about Hailey.

"You could bring her along. Maybe you'll find a grandma whose grandkids are far away."

There were several bunco players who fit that description, and Lily brightened. "What a great idea. Hailey's so cute and good-tempered, everyone will adore her."

"I can't wait to meet her. Speaking of babies, I have exciting news. Ryan and I are pregnant."

"That's wonderful. Congratulations." Lily truly was thrilled for Tina and Ryan, but she was also envious. Would she ever meet the right man and start a family?

They chatted a bit more before Lily announced the purpose of her call. "I'm in trouble," she said. "The IRS is auditing me and I have no idea where to go for help."

The whole thing gave her a bad taste. Needing something to wash it away, she moved purposefully to the refrigerator.

"Gosh, that's scary. You should talk to Ryan. Let me put him on."

While Lily waited, she pulled a bottle of wine from the refrigerator. She took a glass from the cabinet and filled it. There were boxes piled on both bar stools and the armchair in the living room, so she returned to the love seat. She hated the clutter, but there simply was no place to store her jewelry supplies. The building on Main Street had oodles of space behind the retail area at the front—perfect for a workshop. Lily wanted that building.

Seconds later, a deep voice greeted her. "Hello, Lily. Tina tells me you're being audited."

She hastily swallowed a mouthful of wine. "Yes, and I don't know what to do. It's for my tax return from three years ago. I can hardly remember what I did yesterday, let alone back then."

"The first thing you want to do is contact the person who did your taxes that year."

That would be Daryl Chapman, the sculptor she'd been dating at the time. Daryl had claimed to know all about business taxes and tax returns, and when he'd offered to handle Lily's, she'd gladly let him.

Soon after, the relationship had ended. Since then, Lily had filled out the tax forms herself. It was a wonder she wasn't being audited for *those.* She swirled the contents of her glass and sighed. "He left town a good two and a half years ago, and we haven't kept in touch. I don't even know where he is. I'm hoping you can recommend someone local."

"There are several qualified accountants in town, all of them honest," Ryan said. "But the best is a friend of mine, a CPA named Carter Boyle."

Lily recognized the name, but had never met the man. She pictured him to be in his forties with silver streaks in his hair. "I play bunco with his mother, Henri." The woman refused to answer to Mrs. Boyle, saying she felt younger when called by her first name, Henrietta, or her nickname. "Short, midsixties, a real sweetheart? Except during the game. Then she turns into a cutthroat."

"That's Carter's mom, all right. Here's his office number." Ryan gave her the information.

"Thank you," she said. "Congratulations on the pregnancy, and tell Tina I'll see her Saturday night."

## Chapter Two

Sitting behind his desk Thursday afternoon, Carter glanced at his watch. Was it already four forty-five? He frowned.

Looked as if his four o'clock was a no-show. Served him right for taking on a client who wanted him to help her through an audit. A woman he'd never met or worked with. But Ryan Chase had recommended him. Ryan was a good source of referrals, as well as a friend, and Carter didn't want to damage their relationship.

He'd give her five more minutes. If she didn't show, he'd leave, go home and get cleaned up for his date with Heather. Anticipation for the evening ahead—yep, he really was looking forward to tonight—put a smile on his face.

Since her call Monday he'd thought about her a lot. Aside from her physical attributes she was intelligent, with a sense of humor, and if she wanted kids, maybe there was a future with her.

He was cleaning off his desk when Linda buzzed. "Your four o'clock, Lily Gleason, is here."

"Forty-five minutes late," Carter muttered. It was a good thing business had slowed down for the season. Otherwise he'd already be with another client and she wouldn't have gotten in. As it was, he needed to leave in fifteen minutes.

"Should I reschedule her?" Linda asked.

"No, let's get it over with." If Ms. Gleason didn't appreciate cutting their meeting short, too bad. "Send her in."

Moments later she entered his office, her footsteps muffled by the thick beige carpet.

Toting a rosy-cheeked, round-eyed baby with wispy blond hair in one arm and a bulging grocery bag in the other, she headed toward him. With each step her chin-length, curly, light brown hair bounced. *Artsy,* Carter thought, glancing at her striped yellow-and-black tights and what looked like ballet slippers that she wore with a black turtleneck and short yellow jumper. *Bohemian.*

Not at all like the sophisticated women who interested him. Yet strangely, he was attracted to her. But what bothered him was that grocery sack.

"You're younger than I expected." Breathless, she set down the bag and plunked herself and the baby into the chair across the desk. "Sorry I'm late. This is Hailey, my niece—I'm taking care of her for two weeks—and she took a longer than usual nap this afternoon. She woke up cranky, and I had to change and feed her before coming here. I've been looking for a sitter, but I don't exactly know of any, and neither do my friends... But you don't want to hear about that." She tucked her hair behind her ears. In vain. "I'm Lily Gleason."

"Carter Boyle." Resisting the urge to tuck her hair back himself, Carter instead picked up the gold Cross pen a client had given him one Christmas. "I have an appointment out of the office at five forty-five. That gives you and me exactly fourteen minutes. What do you mean, younger?"

"It takes a while to build up a business as successful as yours. I expected a man in his forties."

The compliment pleased Carter, and he straightened his shoulders.

"Ryan Chase says you're honest and straightforward and the best, and that's why I'm here. Are you going to charge me for a full hour?"

The baby—Hailey—regarded Carter with a sober face. He wondered what she was thinking. And couldn't help wondering if at the same age, his own daughter had looked anything like this little one. He had only a single photo of her, taken immediately after her birth. It was tucked in his wallet behind his organ donor card, and he hadn't pulled it out in years. Yet he knew her scrunched-up little face as well as his own. But now was no time to think about her.

He shook his head. "There's no charge for this meeting."

Hailey broke into a gummy grin, as if she understood and approved. "Umpem," she said, then sucked on her fist. Slobber dribbled down her chin.

Slobber aside, she was cute. Carter's chest literally ached. Which was crazy. He'd seen plenty of babies over the years. Why did this particular one remind him of the daughter he'd never had the chance to know?

Because his "baby" had just turned seventeen.

He gave a rotten excuse for a smile. "What'd she just say?"

"That's baby talk for 'whew,'" Lily explained as she extracted a tissue from her enormous black handbag and dabbed at the little mouth.

Focusing on Lily was far easier on the heart. Not bad on the eyes, either. Freckles dusted her cheeks and the bridge of her nose. Charming.

But that grocery bag on the corner of his desk…

Clearly noting his less than thrilled expression, she held him with her big, brown eyes. "You said to bring my records."

For one long moment he lost himself in that gaze. The gold flecks lightened the dark brown to more of a caramel. Unusual color and captivating warmth…

Catching himself, he glanced away. Cleared his throat. "If I spend time sorting through all that," he said, sounding gruff to his own ears, "I'll have to charge extra."

"That's okay. I know I should be more organized." She let out a resigned sigh. "I guess I'd rather be doing other things. I'm an artist. I design and make jewelry for sale."

Yep, he'd been dead-on about the artsy thing. "Tell me more about your business."

"It's called Creations by Lily, and I started it seven years ago. I do all the design work. Two employees help me make the pieces, which I sell in a booth at the waterfront and also on the Internet. Recently I was offered a steal on a brick building just down the street from here. I plan to buy it and establish a permanent location—if the IRS doesn't take everything I own."

A scared look darkened her face. Carter wanted to erase her worries. He wanted that warm expression back. Before he could assure her, she held out her wrist.

"These are a few of mine."

A dozen metal and beaded bracelets jangled pleasantly. Then she fingered the long, dangling beads at her earlobes. Hailey reached for one, but Lily caught her chubby hand and kissed it, diverting her. She was great with the baby.

Carter glanced at the jewelry, but mostly he noted her creamy skin. It looked smooth and soft. And that pink, sensual mouth… "Attractive," he said.

"Thanks. I brought my last three tax returns, like your

secretary said, and the letter from the IRS." She slid the papers out of the handbag.

Carter barely scanned the IRS letter before Lily glanced at the crystal clock on the corner table.

"Oh, dear," she said. "My fourteen minutes are up."

"Fourteen minutes?"

"You have an appointment."

He certainly did. How had he forgotten so quickly? It was the audit, he assured himself, not Lily Gleason. "That's right, I do." Rolling his chair back, he stood.

Lily did the same, Hailey on her hip. The bag of receipts had hidden what was now obvious. Curves. Generous and womanly, enough to stir the interest of any normal, red-blooded male. Willing his body to simmer down, Carter stayed on his side of the desk.

"Will you help me?" she asked, catching her lip—her plump, pink lip—between her teeth.

She was unorganized, messy even. And not punctual. Helping her could be a real time drain. Carter opened his mouth to refer her to someone else. "I'll take a look at these tax returns," he said instead, "and get back to you."

"Thank you *so* much, Mr. Boyle."

She flashed a dazzling smile. Dimples bloomed in each cheek—sweet, tiny symmetrical hollows that bracketed her lips. Holy Hannah.

Like an idiot, he grinned back. "Please call me Carter."

"Carter it is. And you may call me Lily."

She stretched out her arm, the bracelets clinking softly.

He barely had time to note her plain, short nails before his palm slid against hers. She was small-boned, with a firm, callused grip. So different from the smooth, manicured hands of the women he dated. Well, she did make jewelry.

All too soon, she reclaimed her fingers and used them to push the curls from her face. It was no surprise that they quickly sprang back.

"Booly." Hailey squirmed, her face suddenly crumpled in distress.

Worried, Carter peered at her. "She okay?"

"Probably a wet diaper," Lily said, shifting the baby. "When should I come back?"

Carter glanced again at the letter from the IRS. "The audit is roughly seven weeks from now, so we have some breathing room. I'll need time to go through the returns. And that." He nodded at the grocery bag.

Normally he would have stayed late to begin the methodical process of combing through the tax returns and organizing the receipts. But tonight he had a date that could signal the start of a serious relationship.

"How about sometime next week?" he said.

"That'd be great. I'll be on time, I promise, and I'll try to leave Hailey at home. You wouldn't by chance know of a babysitter?"

Carter shook his head. "Afraid not. On your way out, be sure to schedule an appointment with Linda."

"I WAS JUST ABOUT TO CALL you," Charity said when Lily phoned her after Hailey went down for the night. "I can't make the bunco game Saturday night. You'll never guess why."

When either of them had news, they always played the guessing game.

"Hmm…" Seated on the love seat with containers of jewelry supplies beside her—Lily meant to work a few hours—she put her friend on speakerphone, freeing her hands, and began crafting an earring. "You love bunco as much as I do, so it must be something important. A date?"

"Bingo! You won't believe with whom." Charity sounded as giddy as a child on a merry-go-round. "Only Trevor Holt."

The very sexy yacht salesman who custom-ordered a steady supply of Charity's wind socks and chimes. She'd had a crush on him forever. "Ooh, nice going." Even though Charity couldn't see her, Lily gave a thumbs-up. "Tell me more."

"I stopped at the marina this afternoon to deliver an order. As soon as I walked into Trevor's office, he asked me out. Could've knocked me over."

"It's about time. Where's he taking you?"

"We're hopping the ferry to Anacortes to have dinner at this restaurant he really likes. I'm supposed to dress up."

Anacortes was a forty-five-minute ferry ride away. "That sounds fun. I can picture it now—you two standing on the dock, enjoying the sunset. If it doesn't rain."

Even if it poured, the whole thing sounded terribly romantic. Lily hoped that someday some man would take *her* on a romantic ferry ride.

"I'm imagining the same thing, only in my fantasy, Trevor's arms are around me and we're too busy to watch the sunset. I'll let you know how it goes. So, did you find a sitter for Hailey?"

"Not yet, but I refuse to miss bunco." It was only once a month, and Lily enjoyed the socializing too much for that. Besides, Saturday was the one night she totally relaxed, and she wasn't about to sit at home the entire evening. "I figured I'd bring her along—actually, that was Tina Chase's idea. You never know, one of the players might want to babysit, or at least know of someone who could."

"Smart thinking, but isn't Hailey's bedtime eight-thirty? You'll only get to play for an hour."

"That's better than nothing. Wait'll you hear the latest about Tina Chase." Lily was bursting to share the news. "She and Ryan are expecting."

"Really? Wow. She's our age, right?"

"A few years older, I think."

"Then we still have time."

"Of course we do." Lily stopped stringing beads to cross her fingers.

"Speaking of Tina Chase, how was the meeting with that accountant her husband recommended—Carter Boyle?"

Lily thought about the way the accountant had met her gaze directly, a sure sign of an honest man. "I like him. I know he'll be straight with me, no matter what."

"Since he's dealing with your taxes and the IRS, that's good."

"It's good, period. You know I can't tolerate people who lie."

She'd been hurt too many times by her mother's made-up stories, especially those about her father. Telling Lily and Janice he was dead when actually he was alive and well and living in North Seattle, mere miles from them. In a nice house with his wife and son, and wanting nothing to do with his illegitimate daughters. Jerome had fed her more lies, telling her that she was his one and only. Which she'd foolishly believed.

That naive young woman was gone now, replaced by a sadder, wiser one. One with principles she'd never again compromise.

"He doesn't look at all like Henri," she continued. "Where she's a little bit of a thing, he's the opposite—

big and solid-looking. Kind of cute, in a stuffy sort of way." Lily recalled the intelligent glint in his eyes. "He's smart, too, and you should see his offices. They're plush, and so big my whole house could fit inside the reception area."

"If he's doing that well he must be *really* good. Hmm, is he married?"

Lily hadn't noticed a ring—and she'd checked—but not all men wore them. "I don't know. Why, are you interested?"

"In Trevor. I'm thinking about *you*. You're looking for a good man. If he's honest, attractive and successful…"

Lily remembered Carter's less-than-warm expression— except that moment before she'd left, when he'd flashed a genuine smile as he grasped her hand with an oh-so-strong grip. Her heart had seemed to lift in her chest before it fell again. "I don't think I made a very good impression. Hailey took an extra long nap and woke up with an awful mess of a diaper. Then she needed a snack. I was almost an hour late, and he scowled a lot."

"That wasn't your fault! You haven't found a babysitter."

"I know, and I explained that." Lily sighed. "Remember when kids in high school made up an excuse as to why they didn't do their homework, and the teacher didn't buy it? That's how Carter looked at me."

"That sounds cold. Wait, did you say Carter? So you're on a first-name basis."

Charity's speculative tone bothered Lily. "That doesn't mean anything except that we're about the same age." Feeling an odd need to defend the man, she added, "He seemed to think Hailey was cute, so he's not that cold."

"Who wouldn't? She's precious."

"He didn't charge me for the forty-five minutes I

missed, either. *And* he agreed to help me with the audit."
A huge relief.

"Either you're lucky or you charmed him with those
dimples and that wide-eyed look men love."

Having tried both, only to be met with frowns and stiff
shoulders—broad as they were—Lily knew that this male
had not been charmed. He might've cracked the one grin,
but that was probably because the meeting was over.

"Trust me, the man was all business. I did promise to
find a sitter and be on time for our next appointment."

Lily intended to keep her word. The audit loomed like
a dark cloud over her head, and she needed to get on Carter
Boyle's good side.

HEATHER LARKSPUR WAS as attractive as ever. Within ten
minutes of exchanging a brief "hello" kiss that promised
more but did nothing to stir Carter's blood—a bad sign—
they were sipping drinks at a table overlooking the sound
at Harvey's, one of Halo Island's finest restaurants.

"It's good to see you." Heather's smile showed off her
brilliant white teeth, a nice contrast to her burgundy
lipstick. Her dark brown hair was twisted into some kind
of fancy knot. Not a hair out of place. She was trim and
wearing a black dress that clung to her curves, with
tasteful pearl earrings that matched the lovely strand
around her neck.

The opposite of wild-haired, soft-looking Lily Gleason.

Lily hadn't worn lipstick, but oh, that mouth…

"Carter? You're a million miles away." Heather's brow
puckered gently. "If I know you, you're thinking about
one of your clients."

How did she know, and why was he thinking about Lily?

Because tonight was a mistake. He shouldn't have accepted the dinner invitation. But he was a decent man, and he'd see the evening through.

"You're right, I was." He smiled. "I like that dress. You look fantastic."

"Thanks." She met his gaze, then lowered her eyelids a fraction. "You're not bad yourself."

Not long ago he'd have warmed to the sexual undertones with an appropriate comment, setting up a possible night together. Now he ignored her signals and changed the subject. "Still selling real estate?" he asked. They'd met when she sold him his current home.

She nodded. "Last month I was number one in the company."

"Doesn't surprise me. You sure found me the right place. You're the best on the island."

She blinked. Then, to Carter's shock, she teared up. He eyed her warily. "What'd I say?"

"I'm sorry. You're a great guy, and I really wanted to enjoy tonight." Her lower lip trembled. "But I just don't think I'm ready."

Carter's relief that she wasn't interested in him almost drowned out his dismay that she was about to cry. Not sure what to do, he said the only thing that came to mind. "Bad breakup?"

After visibly pulling herself together, she nodded.

"You want to talk about it?"

"I think I do. His name is Austin Crane. He's divorced and lives in Seattle, and I met him when he came to town, looking for a vacation cottage for him and his son. He's handsome and smart, and we just clicked, you know?" Pausing, she fiddled with an earring. "Unfortunately, his four-year-old son never adjusted to me. I don't have much experience with kids, and he must have sensed that I was uncomfortable around him."

She extracted a tissue from a purse a quarter the size of Lily Gleason's and carefully dabbed her eyes. Carter remembered how Lily had fussed over her niece like a loving parent. No discomfort for her.

"Austin and I were together for eight months," Heather continued. "Things were getting serious, and I was even thinking about moving to Seattle. Then a few weeks ago he called to say that he and his wife are getting back together, and that he couldn't see me anymore." She blinked, then sniffled.

"Ouch," Carter said. "I sympathize."

"At least I won't have to deal with his spoiled brat son anymore." She tried to smile.

"See? You found a silver lining."

"I guess I did." She gave Carter a grateful look. "Thanks for letting me share my sad story, Carter. You always were a good listener."

"And you're a class act. I've always thought so."

"That means a lot. You and I used to have so much fun together. Why didn't we ever get serious?"

"At the time neither of us was ready."

"Austin made me feel ready, but now… I'm starting to wonder if I'll ever meet my soul mate."

"I hear you. Lately I've been thinking about settling down myself," Carter admitted. "But like you, I haven't met the right woman."

"A fine pair we are. Let's make a toast." Heather raised her glass and so did Carter. "To both of us. May we each find our life partner someday soon."

"Amen," Carter said. They clinked rims and drank.

"Enough of this somber talk for one evening." Heather's eyes glinted with determination. "Let's enjoy dinner as the friends we are."

So they did. As the meal wound to a close, she laughed at one of Carter's jokes. He thought again of Lily, wondered how she looked and sounded when she laughed. Her eyes probably sparkled and her cheeks flushed. It was only a quick leap to fantasizing about her in the throes of passion. He pictured her soft and restless under him.

Now *that* got his body seriously interested, especially a certain part of his anatomy. Over a woman he barely knew, a client. Carter didn't get romantically involved with his clients. Besides, a natural beauty like Lily probably had a boyfriend. And he was through thinking about her.

At the end of the evening he drove Heather home. Clouds hung in the dark night sky, the air smelled of the sea and a fine mist swirled in the headlights.

"Bet there's a halo over the sound tonight," he said. The island was named for the halo-shaped fog that often hovered over the water.

"I love these misty, foggy nights—they're great for snuggling," Heather said, sounding wistful. "Luckily, I have my two cats."

Carter didn't even have *one*. As he parked in Heather's driveway, she touched his arm.

"Thanks for tonight. I'm glad we did this." She leaned over and kissed his cheek. "You take care, and remember, she's out there."

Later, standing in the middle of his spacious, state-of-the-art kitchen, he glanced at the tastefully painted walls and the high-end table and chairs that looked so good, courtesy of a professional decorator. Everything neat and in its place, exactly as he liked it.

The rest of his four-bedroom home was equally beautiful, something to be proud of. Trouble was, the house felt empty.

A woman would change that. Carter thought about how to find the right one for him. Not so easy on the island, where there weren't all that many single females his age. Maybe he'd sign up with one of those matchmaking groups on the Internet, or put a personal ad in the paper. But several of his buddies had tried both, with dismal results. He thought about asking his friends to fix him up, but that could be equally disastrous. Besides, his mother might find out, and the way she liked to stick her nose into his business… She'd either nag him to death or try to set him up with this or that friend's daughter.

Carter winced at the thought.

Hell, maybe he'd just get a dog.

## Chapter Three

By Saturday morning Lily was bleary-eyed. There was tons to do, and with Hailey taking up so much of her time... Something had to give, and it was sleep.

Now, at the crack of dawn, she sipped coffee and printed out Joyce and Cindy's time sheets for the previous two weeks. In the days since her birthday lunch, they'd both put in extra hours, for which Lily was grateful. Without them, she'd be in a world of trouble.

She just hoped that the audit went well and she could continue to employ them.

The instant the *A* word popped into her head, she clenched her teeth. Then she thought about Carter Boyle. Since their appointment she'd done that a lot. Ryan had said he was the best CPA around, honest and straightforward. Knowing he'd help her lifted a huge weight from her shoulders.

There were other reasons why Carter filled her thoughts. Even though she'd met him only once and they'd talked a mere fourteen minutes, strictly business, she knew without a doubt that he was a good man, the kind she'd wished for when she blew out her birthday candles.

She suspected that, tax expertise aside, Carter Boyle excelled at many things. Kissing, for one…

Lily couldn't stem a dreamy sigh. She was definitely attracted to the man. Which was a waste of time, for as she'd told Charity, he'd shown no interest in her except as a client. No doubt he was married or seriously involved with someone really special. Lily imagined his lover as well-dressed and sophisticated, with long legs and nice, straight hair that never curled or got in her eyes. A woman with more than a community college arts degree in jewelry and metal design, who'd probably never been late in her life.

For a moment her spirits plummeted. But there was no sense dwelling on her own shortcomings—or Carter or the audit. She was far too busy for that. After cutting paychecks and popping them into envelopes to mail, Lily printed out yesterday's Internet orders, which needed to be packed and shipped. She really ought to hire someone to handle this side of the business during tourist season. Even more critical, she still needed a sitter for the next ten or so days. But who?

Baby noises floated toward her. Hailey was awake. Every morning she woke up gurgling and happy, a real day brightener. Despite her fatigue and worries, Lily couldn't help smiling.

As she changed the baby's diaper, she told her about the morning ahead. "After breakfast, we'll visit my booth off Front Street." One of three dozen near the waterfront that sold local crafts to the vast hordes of summer visitors. The company that owned the booths handled the maintenance on the roof and structure, but the renters maintained the interiors. "It needs a thorough cleaning and a fresh coat of paint, and you get to sit in your stroller and watch me make it pretty."

Hailey blew bubbles and laughed.

After Lily fed, bathed and dressed her, activities that always took longer than anticipated, she grabbed her cleaning supplies and a bulging diaper bag, having quickly learned to pack extra clothes, diapers, bottles, baby food and toys. She propped her niece on her hip and rubbed noses with her. "Time to head out. It's too early now, but when we get back, we'll call your mommy."

Who hadn't phoned in almost a week, since Lily's birthday on Monday. This really bothered Lily. And worried her. Didn't Janice wonder how Hailey was doing? Did she care about her at all?

"Fum," Hailey replied, waving her arms.

Which Lily interpreted to mean, "Oh, goody, let's go."

Three hours later, grimy and worn-out, the booth clean but not yet painted—who could paint with a seven-month-old baby fussing for attention?—Lily wheeled the stroller back across Whaler's Wharf Lane, which was more like a short dirt driveway, toward the long dock the locals referred to as Houseboat Row. Ten houseboats, including hers, were anchored there.

It was a balmy afternoon, with not a cloud to be seen. Lily raised her face to the warm sun and made her way slowly over the packed dirt. By the time she reached the dock, Hailey was asleep. Which was a shame, since the view from here was spectacular. The water sparkled. Everyone had planted flowers in pots, and the dock was awash in color. The floral scents mingled with the salty smell of the sea—how Lily loved that!—and she inhaled appreciatively. Several artists besides Lily lived on Houseboat Row, and many of the homes bore unique artistic touches—a hand-forged, wrought-iron peace symbol here, a hanging jute weaving there.

She saw Mr. Creech and his leashed pug, Philomena, making their way slowly toward her, and waved. "Isn't it a great day for a walk!"

"About time the weather cleared up," he said in his brusque way.

He peered at Hailey, who, with her lips parted and her lashes dark against her rosy cheeks, looked like a little angel. Lily's heart swelled with love, and Mr. Creech's old weathered face softened in a tender smile. "I see it's nap time."

"For the next few hours, if I'm lucky." Lily stooped to rub between Philomena's ears, for which she earned a warm lick on her hand. "I spent this morning cleaning my booth. Hailey was so good. She seemed fascinated, and I had the feeling she wanted to help. But she started fussing before I could paint, so I'll have to go back another day. How's Patsy?" Mr. Creech's daughter lived with her husband and kids in Spokane, several hundred miles away.

"Just talked to her this morning." His smile dimmed. "She's pressuring me to move to Spokane now. But I told her, not until I sell the building and my houseboat. Realtor's coming Monday to look at the houseboat."

"Oh. That's fast." Had he changed his mind about waiting until fall? Lily hoped not. "Does this mean you want the down payment now? Because I need a little more time."

"If it were anybody else, I would. But you've always been good to me, sometimes better than Patsy. I want you to have the building. As long as you have the money by the end of September."

"I will." Lily wasn't about to mention the audit, for fear he'd change his mind. Then her conscience pricked her— she was not like her mother or Janice, and would not withhold the truth, no matter what the consequences. "That is, I hope to have it by then," she said. "You should know that I'm about to be audited."

Mr. Creech squinted at her, his mouth turning down at the corners. "What does that mean?"

"Probably nothing," she stated, doing her best to sound confident. "I'll know for sure by mid to late June."

"You'll tell me if you can't come up with the money?"

At those dire words her mouth went dry. Gripping the stroller handle, she nodded.

Philomena began to whine, her leash straining as she tried to move forward. "All right, all right," Mr. Creech said. "Best get going. Keep me posted on that audit."

"Absolutely."

Refusing to ruin the flawless day with worries about the IRS, Lily hummed as she wheeled the stroller home. Beside her front door, the magenta-and-yellow wind sock Charity had traded for a necklace flapped gaily in the breeze.

Leaving the stroller outside, she carefully transported Hailey to her crib. Then it was time to call Janice. Lily headed purposefully for her cell phone. After eight rings Janice's voice mail picked up.

Lily waited for the beep, then left her message. "It's Lily. Hailey's wonderful, but she needs her mommy. I'm counting on you to be here a week from Sunday, Wednesday at the latest. Because on Thursday my booth opens for the summer. Once that happens, I positively, absolutely cannot take care of her. Call me."

IT WAS CARTER'S TURN to host the monthly Saturday night poker game, which coincided with bunco night. Cards, poker chips and ashtrays sat on the dining-room table. The fridge was stocked with beer and snacks, and Carter looked forward to an evening of laughs and good fun.

Two of his poker buddies, D. J. Hatcher and Ryan Chase, were already here, along with their wives, Liza and Tina. The ladies wouldn't stay long. As soon as the last player, Alex Frost, Carter's oldest friend on the island, and his new bride, Ginny, showed up, the women would head for their bunco game at the community center. Then Carter and his buds would bring out the cigars and the raunchier sides of their personalities and get down to the serious business of playing poker.

While waiting for Alex and Ginny, Carter ushered his guests into the spacious living room with huge windows that faced a large deck and the water. In a few weeks he'd open the slider, but it wasn't warm enough yet.

"Can I get anyone a drink or something to eat?" he asked.

Liza shook her head. "We're saving up for the goodies at bunco."

"I so love your house," Tina said. "Just look at this room. The plush cream carpet, high, beamed ceilings and that view of the water and the islands… Spectacular."

Carter liked his house, too, especially when it was filled with friends. "If you and Ryan are interested, there's a view lot up the way for sale."

Ryan glanced at his wife. "Say the word and I'll build you a house out here."

"Leave G.G. and Huckleberry Hill Road?" His wife looked appalled. "I could never do that. Especially now." She touched her as-yet flat belly.

G.G. was like a grandmother to Tina, and Tina and Ryan lived across the street from her in a tight-knit neighborhood. Carter didn't blame them for wanting to stay put.

"Anytime you need a water fix you're welcome to stop by our house," Liza said. She and D.J. owned a sweet little cottage right on the beach a few miles down the road.

"Thanks." Tina turned to Carter. "What I meant was that someday some lucky lady will be very happy here. If you ever decide to settle down."

Carter hadn't told anyone that he was looking to do just that, but he had nothing to hide. "Funny you mention that because I've been thinking about it lately. I'm ready to find the right woman."

Tina grinned and Liza threw him a thumbs-up. Carter frowned. "Whatever you do, don't say anything to my mother. You know how she is."

"Mum's the word," Liza said.

Tina pretended to lock her lips. "Speaking of finding your soul mate, how was your date with Heather?"

The four of them eyed Carter with interest. Did they all know about that? Well, he *had* mentioned it to D.J. during their appointment the other day.

"She's just out of a relationship, and there's no chemistry." He shrugged.

"That's the breaks," D.J. said.

His wife gave Carter a sympathetic look. "At least now you know she isn't right for you. Better sooner than later."

A woman who'd been stood up at the altar, she ought to know. Three years later she'd married D.J. and now they were Mr. and Mrs. Happy.

"I wish I could think of someone to fix you up with," Liza said. "Tina? Does anyone come to mind?"

Carter thought about getting to know a certain some-one—Lily Gleason. An idea he promptly dismissed. Only to visualize a series of blind dates from hell, set up by his well-meaning friends. He glanced at D.J. and Ryan. Both looked as if they wanted to say something, but neither did. They knew which side of the bed they slept on.

"I appreciate the offer," he said. "But I don't need any help."

"If you're sure…" Tina looked skeptical. "Because between the two of us and Ginny, I know we could come up with some possible—"

The doorbell chimed, cutting her off.

Thank God. Carter gave his brow a mental swipe. "There's Alex." He strode toward the door.

Five minutes later the women left. Carter and his buddies ambled into the dining room, where he passed out cigars and beer, then set out the food. With matches flaring and smoke billowing, he and his friends took their seats around the table.

"You really don't want our wives to fix you up," D.J. said as he puffed on his cigar. "Much as I love mine…" A smirk tugged his lips. "You never know who they'll come up with."

Alex scooped up a handful of mixed nuts. "Man, if they fix you up, you'll be swimming in dangerous waters, for sure. What if you didn't like the person they chose?"

"Amen," Ryan said. "I'm crazy about Tina, and I trust her completely. But fixing up a friend is right up there with taking ballroom dance lessons."

Which Tina had given him for Christmas last year.

"I'm with you there." Carter set his cigar in an ashtray. He picked up the deck of cards and shuffled. "But, hell, I'd really like to meet someone, and I don't want to put an ad in the paper. Five card draw all right to start with?"

His friends nodded. Ryan cut the cards.

"Why not just relax and let it happen?" D.J. suggested. "You know, continue to play the field."

As Carter dealt the cards, he thought about the many years he'd spent dating, and knew he didn't want that anymore. "I could," he said.

"You should." Alex anted up three red chips. "Don't get me wrong—marriage is great. But until I met Ginny, I didn't really think about it."

Recently, Carter had thought about it a lot. He tossed in the same number and color of chips, then glanced around the table. "Unless I'm missing something, marriage has done you three a world of good."

"It sure has," Alex said. "I've never been happier than these past six weeks." With a self-satisfied smile, he picked up his cards and studied them. Then he tossed two blue chips onto the mound in the center of the table. "I'll raise you."

"You'll be sorry." D.J. added his two blue chips to the rest. "You're right about marriage, Carter. I wouldn't trade being married to Liza for anything. She makes everything I do worth the effort."

"I couldn't have said it better." Ryan slid his chips to the center of the table. "Tina's the best thing that ever happened to me and Maggie. And now that we're expecting… There's nothing like making a baby with the woman you love."

Carter wondered about his own daughter, somewhere out there. Did she feel hurt that he wasn't in her life? The thought was painful, so instead he pictured two little Boyles who both looked like him scampering through the house. Only that wasn't quite right. One had out-of-control curly hair and dimples like Lily Gleason's.

He barely knew the damned woman, yet here she was in his head again. Having his kids. He frowned. "Let's not talk about this anymore, huh? Lay down your cards, men, and prepare to lose. 'Cause I have something you can't beat—a straight flush."

His buddies groaned and swore. Triumphant, Carter raked the chips toward him. Puffed on his cigar, and got down to the business of enjoying himself.

THANKS TO HAILEY'S sudden whim to rub strained peas in her hair and ears, which led to a bath, Lily was almost late for bunco, where women went as much to socialize as to play the game. In the year since bunco night had started, the monthly event had grown in popularity. Now some twenty-odd women of various ages gathered at five or six tables, where they played two separate games at the same time. As Lily pushed the stroller into the community center rec room, laughter and conversation filled the air.

Smiling, she waved at friends and acquaintances, most of whom looked surprised to see her with a baby. Well, the story would get around soon enough. With any luck, by the end of the evening she'd have a sitter or two lined up. With that in mind she'd dressed Hailey in a pair of pink overalls, a pink polka-dot turtleneck and the cutest little ruffled pink socks. She was so adorable that everyone would fall in love with her.

Grabbing a handful of peanut M&M's from the laden food table, Lily let her gaze travel the room in search of an empty seat. She spotted Tina sitting with Liza, Ginny and another woman, and headed over to say hello and spread the word.

"This is Hailey, my sister's little one," she said, bending down to pull up one sock.

On cue, the baby laughed. "Oolee," she said, kicking her legs. She seemed to have no problems with the high noise level.

"She's so cute!" Liza gushed.

Ginny grinned at Hailey, then sighed. "Makes me want a baby right away, even if I am a newlywed."

With a Mona Lisa smile, Tina covered her slightly rounded abdomen with her palm. "I only have to wait another six and a half months. May I hold her?" She was practically salivating.

"Of course, but if I don't find a seat right away, I may not be able to play. Maybe during the break? But I should warn you, Hailey's bedtime is eight-thirty. She might be crabby."

"If not tonight, some other time," Tina said.

"Great. If you all would pass the word that I need someone to watch her for about the next nine or so days, I'd appreciate it."

Lily spied an empty seat in the back corner and moved that way. The three women at the table were older than her, and one of them was Henri Boyle. Well, wasn't that interesting, and the perfect way to find out more about Carter. Such as whether he was married or romantically involved with anyone.

"Hello," Lily said. "I'm only here until the first break, but may the baby and I join you?"

All three women nodded welcomes.

"Who have we here?" Henri asked, smiling at Hailey.

Who flashed her gums right back.

"This is my niece, Hailey."

"Aren't you the sweetest thing," crooned Rose Thorne, a slender, gray-haired woman. "How old is she?"

"Seven months. I'm watching her while my sister is…traveling."

Betty Jackson, who ran the post office, leaned toward Hailey and cooed. "My son and his wife in Anacortes are expecting their first, and I can hardly wait. Once that baby arrives, you can bet I'll be visiting every chance I get."

"May I hold her?" Henri asked.

"It's okay with me." Lily looked at Hailey. "Do you mind if Henri holds you?"

"Flubee."

"I think that means she likes the idea," Lily said, and her tablemates chuckled.

Her face wistful—no doubt she wanted a grandchild of her own—Henri settled Hailey on her lap. "I'd forgotten how lovely babies smell. I wish…" For a moment sorrow etched her face. Then it was gone. "Never mind."

Had something sad happened to a child in her life? Lily wanted to know, but she and Henri weren't close enough for her to ask. "You're Carter's mother," she said.

"That I am." Behind her bifocals she had the same sky-blue eyes as Carter. Only hers sparkled with warmth and humor. His had been serious and focused. "I didn't realize you knew my son."

"We met last week. He's going to help me with a tax situation." Lily bit her lip. "I'm being audited. Not me personally—my company."

"Your jewelry business?" Betty frowned. "That's not good. A few years ago a friend of mine who owns a tourist shop on one of the other islands was audited."

"How did it go?" Lily asked.

Betty gave her head a dire shake. "You don't want to know."

Not what Lily wanted to hear. The M&M's she'd eaten felt leaden in her stomach, and she bit her lip.

"You're scaring the poor girl." Henri smiled at Lily. "Don't you worry. If anyone can help you, Carter can."

Hailey grabbed on to Henri's watch, but the older woman didn't seem to mind. "He's the best accountant around. And I don't say that because he's my son."

Lily couldn't imagine her mother ever saying anything so nice about her or Janice. "Carter's lucky to have such a wonderful, supportive mother," she said. "I'll bet his wife loves you."

"Oh, he isn't married. No girlfriend right now, either."

This was both a relief and a surprise. "Oh," Lily said.

"All his friends are married now. Tonight he's playing poker with three of them—Ryan Chase, D. J. Hatcher and Alex Frost. They're probably smoking smelly cigars and swearing up a storm. You know how men are. I'm sure their wives are grateful for our bunco game."

Carter played poker? Lily couldn't imagine Mr. Serious smoking cigars and swearing. She found the image intriguing. "Really," she said, then glanced at the round wall clock. Time was slipping by, and she was no closer to finding a sitter. She had to be a little more direct. "Hailey will be here for another week and a half," she began.

"How lovely," Rose said, then looked at her tablemates. "Seems like we're off to a late start tonight. I think I'll make a quick run to the snack table."

"I'll come with you," Betty said. "Who wants goodies?"

"Me." Henri kissed the baby's round little head. "Lily?"

"A fudge brownie, please."

As soon as Rose and Betty left, Henri peered at Lily. "Tell me, dear, are you seeing anyone special?"

"Not at the moment."

"Why not? You're a darling."

Lily felt her face flush. She fiddled with a curl. "Thank you. I *was* involved with someone, but there was this little problem—he was a liar." She saw no reason to tell Carter Boyle's mother any more than that.

"Then I'm glad it ended. Honesty is so important in a relationship. You deserve better."

"Thank you." Uncomfortable with the woman's scrutiny, Lily changed the subject. "As I was saying before, Hailey will be with me for another week or so, and I'm looking for someone to watch her while I get ready for the tourist season. I'll pay well, so if you know of—"

"We're back," Rose said as she and Betty returned with popcorn and a paper plate piled with brownies and napkins. "Did we miss anything?"

"Oh, this and that." Henri patted Hailey's back and looked at Lily. "I was about to say that my son is what we women call a good catch. So far, though, no one has managed to hook him. What he needs is for a very special person to come into his life and make him want to settle down."

And she was telling Lily this because? Henri couldn't possibly think that Carter…with Lily… Except as a client, the man was not interested in her. If he knew what his mother was doing, he'd probably throw a fit.

All three women were looking at Lily, seemingly waiting for her response. She took her time finishing her mouthful of brownie. "When he's ready, I'm sure it'll happen."

At last Margie Best, the woman in charge of bunco night, made her way to the front of the room. The games were about to begin. It was time for Lily to make her request.

"If you three could spread the word that I need a sitter, I'd really appreciate it."

"I could watch her," Henri said.

Lily knew she looked surprised. "You could? That'd be great. She's a lot of work, though."

"You have no idea how long I've wanted to spoil a grandbaby." That wistful expression returned. Henri's arms tightened a fraction around Hailey, who looked blissfully content. "Spending time with this little one will be an absolute treat."

"Are you sure? It'll be a minimum of six hours per day, probably more. Even with Hailey's two-hour afternoon nap, that's a big chunk of energy and time."

"I'm willing to give it a try. Besides, it's only for a short while."

"Then we have a deal. I really appreciate this."

Henri's broad smile said it all.

"Good evening, everyone," Margie greeted the group. "Ready to play some bunco?"

Henri leaned toward Lily. "Shall I come to your house?" she whispered in a loud voice.

"That's not necessary," Lily replied softly, knowing she'd never find an hour or thirty to tidy up. "My place is really tiny. It'd be best if I brought Hailey to you. How about Monday morning?"

"Wonderful. I think we should give Hailey a chance to get used to me and my house. Carter's coming over for dinner tomorrow night. Why don't you two join us? Six o'clock?"

The very thought of dinner with Carter at his mother's house flustered Lily. She opened her mouth. "I—"

"All right, ladies, roll those dice!" Margie said.

"Six o'clock tomorrow," Henri repeated.

She rolled the dice, and the matter was closed.

## Chapter Four

Every Sunday Carter's mother cooked him dinner, an evening they both enjoyed. It gave them a chance to catch up on things and spend a few hours together. After reviewing Lily Gleason's tax returns and sorting through her bag of receipts all afternoon, he was ready to push her from his mind and focus on his mother's life. Lily occupied his thoughts far more than any other client, and constant reminders that she was his client and he barely knew her didn't help at all.

As he turned onto his mother's street, he thought about what he'd learned from Lily's tax returns. Her small business was profitable and growing steadily. She'd actually managed to put money into savings. Having seen more than a few small businesses start off with promise, only to fail, Carter was impressed. Lily might seem like a disorganized artist, but she was one sharp businesswoman. Sexy, too. That curvy body was made for pleasure, and he imagined her pressed tight against him, her kissable mouth hungry under his…. Carter groaned out loud. What he wouldn't give to find out…

He stifled that train of thought and pulled to a stop in

front of his mother's little white bungalow. Fantasies would get him nowhere but frustrated. It was five minutes to six. Time to focus on dear old Mom. On dinner.

She was a great cook, and Carter was hungry. She hadn't told him what she was making, but she'd asked him to pick up a bottle of red wine, though she usually didn't drink at dinner. Since she rarely asked him to bring anything, he was happy to contribute. Tucking the bottle under his arm, he strode up the concrete walkway.

His mother had always enjoyed gardening, and this year's spring flowers waved from the beds lining both sides of the walkway. Carter didn't know their names, but they were colorful and cheery and made the air smell sweet. More spilled from the planter under the living-room window, brightening up what was left of the damp, overcast day.

He climbed the three concrete steps to the little porch. Wiped his feet on the welcome mat, and without knocking opened the door. As he stepped into the tiny parquet entry, delicious aromas floated toward him.

Carter sniffed appreciatively. "Hey, Mom," he called out.

"In the kitchen."

Mouth watering, he headed down the hall, past the powder room and into the old but comfortable kitchen. Her face flushed from the heat, his mother stood at the stove holding a large spoon. Her striped bib apron was spattered with tomato sauce.

"Sure smells good in here," he said, noting her pleased smile. "I picked up that wine you wanted." He held up the bottle.

"Merlot. Perfect. Set it on the counter, will you? And then…" She pointed at her cheek and raised it for a kiss.

Carter bent down and quickly brushed the soft skin. A

pot of water was about to boil. Licking his lips, he lifted the lid of the pan simmering on the stove.

"My favorite spaghetti sauce." The stuff took all day to cook, and she usually only made it on his birthday, which was in October. That and the wine made him wonder what she was up to. "What's the occasion?" he asked.

A guilty expression crossed her face. He narrowed his eyes. "If you're trying to cheer me up because my daughter's seventeenth birthday was Monday…" Saying it out loud was painful. "Don't."

"As if food and wine could make either of us feel better."

She looked hurt, which made him feel like a jerk. He kicked at the linoleum. "Shouldn't have said that. Guess I'm a little sensitive."

"It's all right, son. This time of year, we both are."

A dark cloud seemed to fill the kitchen, and for a long moment they were silent. The gurgle of rapidly boiling water broke the spell.

"The water's ready." His mother fed a large quantity of dry spaghetti noodles into the pot.

That and the amount of sauce puzzled Carter. "You're making enough for six people. I know the leftovers are great, but this much?"

"We're having company. Two guests."

His mother was faced away from him, busy putting garlic bread into the oven, but Carter caught her sly expression. What was going on here? He recalled last night's conversation with his buddies and their wives before the women left for bunco. They all knew he wanted to meet someone. If Ginny, Tina or Liza had said something to his mother…

But they'd promised to keep their mouths shut, and Carter was pretty sure he could trust them. Couldn't he?

Wary, he eyed his mother. Wait, she'd said *two* guests. That didn't sound like a blind date. Unless… Carter canted his hip against the counter and crossed his arms. "Tell me you didn't invite a single woman and her mother."

"Not exactly," his mother said, but her refusal to meet his eyes belied the words.

"You did." He groaned. "Dammit, Mom." Ignoring her shocked glance—she didn't like it when he swore, but at this moment Carter didn't care—he mentally ran through the possibilities. "It's one of the women you quilt with, isn't it?" He recalled something about her friend Eugenia Phillips, and her about to turn thirty-five single daughter, Delores… "It's the Phillipses, isn't it?" Just thinking of the beak-nosed woman and her thin-lipped, whiny daughter made him shudder. "You can tell them I'm sick, because I'm out of here." He glanced at his watch. It was nearly six-thirty. "They're late. I hope there's still time to escape."

As he pushed away from the counter, his mother waved her spoon at him. "Delores Phillips? Think, son! The very thought of her as a daughter-in-law… It's enough to ruin my appetite for a week."

That was a relief. "Then who'd you invite?" Carter asked. "Did Tina, Liza or Ginny mention that I'm ready to get married and settle down?"

"No, but I'm awfully glad to hear that. It's about time." She wiped her hands on her apron and shot a worried glance toward the door. "I wish you'd told me sooner. Who is she?"

Then she hadn't known, after all. Carter cursed himself for sharing his plans. "Haven't met her yet. And I want you to stay out of it. That means no trying to fix me up, and no inviting single women to Sunday dinner without checking with me first."

Her eyes widened. "All right, but it's too late—"

At the staccato rap of the brass door knocker she broke off. "There are our guests. Why don't you let them in?"

"I'd rather slip out the back," he said, sounding to his own ears like a willful teenage boy. Somehow his mother had reduced him to that. "But I'll stay."

Rolling his eyes, he headed for the front door. When he opened it, Lily Gleason and Hailey stood there. They were the last people he expected, and he couldn't hide his surprise. "Lily. What are *you* doing here?"

"I guess your mom didn't tell you." She was wearing another jumper, this one navy. With a snug red T-shirt underneath. And long, dangly earrings. Her big brown eyes searched his. "She invited us last night, when we shared her bunco table. She's going to babysit Hailey, and thought I should bring her over to get used to the house."

"She *what?*" Gaping like a fool, Carter tried to imagine his mother taking care of Lily's niece. Why hadn't she told him?

"Don't worry, it's only for a week or so, until my sister picks her up. I'm paying her."

Lily's smooth brow wrinkled and her mouth formed a slight pucker. That drew his attention to her plump, pink lips. He smelled lilacs—not from the bush out front, but from her.

The desire he'd fought all day—actually, since he'd first met her—flared with a vengeance. And he knew he was in trouble. "It's not about money," he said, willing his body to behave. His father had left his mother with enough to live comfortably for the rest of her life.

"Pff," Hailey said, beaming and stretching her hand out as if she remembered and liked him.

"Hello there, pip-squeak," he said, tweaking her little nose. *Pip-squeak?*

His mother headed toward him, frowning. The apron was gone and she'd combed her hair. "For heaven's sake, Carter, let them in."

Both looking forward to and dreading the night ahead, he stepped back and gestured Lily and the baby inside.

SEATED AT ONE END of the rectangular dining-room table, Henri set down her dessert fork. She smiled at Carter at the opposite end, then at Lily and Hailey. "More pie, anyone?"

Lily glanced at Carter, who frowned, and not for the first time tonight. Between his silence and Henri's almost too warm attention, the meal had been less than comfortable.

"None for me, thanks," he said.

Lily shook her head. "Me, either. But it was delicious." The homemade chocolate pecan pie had melted in her mouth. Hailey had enjoyed her small taste, too. And had gobbled up her spaghetti, which Henri had thoughtfully purified in the blender. "The whole meal was outstanding. I wish I could cook like you."

"Your mother didn't teach you?"

"Her idea of cooking was to open a box of macaroni and cheese."

"I could teach you."

"Really? I've always wanted to learn."

Carter made a choking sound, which indicated what he thought of *that* idea. It was more than obvious he didn't like Lily here, and certainly didn't want his mother giving her cooking lessons. Her spirits plummeted. She should never have accepted Henri's dinner invitation.

"Unfortunately, this is a really busy time of year for me so I really can't. Maybe sometime in the future." Lily folded her napkin. "I should take Hailey home now."

As if she'd been cued, the baby began to fuss and pull on her hair.

His face filled with concern, Carter eyed Lily's niece. "Are you tired, pip-squeak? Don't worry, your aunt Lily's about to take you home."

"You can't leave yet." Henri fluttered her hand in the dismissive wave Lily had seen at bunco when she was on a winning streak and didn't want to break. "She'll be up for another hour yet, won't she, Lily? She likely wants to get down and roll around on the living-room floor."

That was probably true, and in Henri's house, there was actually room to do that. Lily darted a glance at Carter.

"Don't look at me," he said, sending his mother a dagger glare.

"It'll give me a chance to play with Hailey, and give her a chance to get familiar with me and the living room," Henri insisted.

She really wanted them to stay, so Lily shrugged. "All right, but just for a little while longer." The baby's face, hands and hair were a mess of spaghetti sauce. "I'd better clean her up first." Lily scooted back her chair and started to stand.

"I'll do it," Henri said. "It's good practice. You sit here and keep Carter company."

As soon as Henri lifted Hailey from the high chair she'd borrowed, and they left the dining room, Lily leaned toward Carter. "I think your mother's trying to fix us up," she said in a low voice.

"No kidding," he replied in equally soft tones. "Whatever you two talked about last night, she's got it in her head that we should get together." His pained expression told Lily what he thought of that idea.

She understood. Nobody appreciated a matchmaking mother. Especially when the attraction was purely one-sided.

Carter wasn't attracted to her. If only she felt the same. But the longer she sat here, the more she liked Carter Boyle—despite his scowls. At least he was honest about his feelings.

Lily tried to recall last night's conversation. "All I said was that you're handling my audit and that I need a sitter for Hailey." She remembered something else, too. "She did ask if I was single."

"Are you?"

She nodded and glanced at his face to see if she could figure out what he was thinking. But his expression gave nothing away.

"There you go," he said.

"I never dreamed she wanted to fix us up. I guess she wants you to find someone, and this is her way of helping."

"I don't *need* her help."

"At least she cares," Lily said. "My mother's so wrapped up in herself and whoever she's dating, she'd never even think of trying to fix me up. It's been weeks since I heard from her." Still no birthday card.

"Mine hasn't looked at a man since my dad died ten years ago. That's probably why she's so interested in me." Carter's mouth quirked. "Maybe we should trade."

It was the closest to a smile he'd cracked all evening, and Lily was glad to see it. Elbow on the table, chin on her fist, she smiled back. "Believe me, you're better off with Henri. And I appreciate her help. With her looking after Hailey I'll be on time for our appointment Tuesday morning."

The living room was only a short distance away, and she could hear the baby and Henri making noises at each other.

Carter shook his head. "She really likes your niece."

"The feeling's mutual. I think she wants a grandchild."

Grief momentarily darkened Carter's face, just as it had Henri's last night. Lily wanted to know why, but it wasn't her business, so she didn't ask. She was glad that Henri had Hailey to love, even if it was only for a short time.

"I looked over your records today," Carter said.

"On a Sunday? Wow, that's dedication."

Lily worked Sundays, too, from April through September. She and Carter were a lot alike, she decided. Both of them were hard workers and honest. Oh, she liked him.

"I'd like to see the booth where you sell your jewelry," he said. "To get a feel for the setup. I'm thinking we should spend part of our meeting there."

"Okay." She'd definitely paint and fix up the interior tomorrow. Remembering what Rose had said about a friend's bad audit, Lily bit her lip. "Tell me the truth, Carter. What are my chances with the audit?"

His attention homed in on her mouth. "That all depends."

"On what?"

He didn't seem to hear her, just continued to stare at her lips with an unreadable expression.

Maybe she had chocolate on them. Lily licked them clean, but didn't taste anything. Carter made a soft sound in his throat, puzzling her.

"Is there something wrong with my mouth?" she asked.

His eyelids lowered a fraction. "Not a thing."

That avid expression made her feel warm inside. Apparently he *was* attracted to her after all. The instant she formed the thought his face tensed and he looked away.

"I always do the dishes and clean up the kitchen." He rose. "Best get started."

None of Lily's boyfriends had ever voluntarily offered to clean up after a meal. Impressed, she, too, stood and began stacking plates. "I'll help."

"I won't try to talk you out of that. Would you rather wash or dry?"

"Dry," she said.

"Deal."

As the sink filled with water and suds, Carter rolled up his sleeves. Lily had never really noticed a man's wrists before. Carter's were thick and masculine and oh, so sexy. Who'd have thought that part of a guy could be so fascinating? Stifling a sigh, she loaded the dishwasher with plates, glasses and silverware.

Standing beside each other, she and Carter tackled the pots and pans, their conversation relaxed and easy. He was a good six inches taller than her, and beside him she felt small and protected. Which was silly, since she didn't need his protection. This close, she could smell his spicy aftershave. His long fingers skilfully wielded the scouring pad and made quick work of the spaghetti pot. She imagined those hands touching her with the same skill. Her nerves began to thrum and she swallowed.

No doubt about it, she had a major crush on Carter Boyle.

"Where exactly is Hailey's mother?" he asked over the hiss of the water.

"Janice is touring with her boyfriend. He's in a rock band and they're letting her sing backup. She'll be here a week from Wednesday at the latest." Lily hoped. She still hadn't heard from her sister and was beginning to worry.

"What about the father?"

"Out of the picture. I think it's sad that he'll never get to know Hailey, but apparently he doesn't care. Some men are like that." Lily's father certainly had been. She shook her head. "If they don't want children, why aren't they more careful?"

In the instant of silence following her words, a muscle in Carter's jaw ticced. "Because accidents happen. Did you ever stop to think that maybe the father wants to be involved in his daughter's life but Janice won't let him?"

He sounded angry. Suddenly the very air felt tense. Lily had offended him, but she had no idea why.

"Believe me, Janice would love for him to take a role in Hailey's life," she answered. "He's not interested in seeing his daughter or helping Janice financially. In fact, after she told him she was pregnant, he left town. She doesn't even know where he is."

His expression grim, Carter said nothing. So Lily went on. "Not all men are as responsible as you."

A haunted look crossed his face, but was gone so fast she was certain she'd misread it. He didn't quite meet her eye as he handed her a freshly rinsed saucepan, confusing her even more.

"I know from experience," she said, rushing to fill the awkward silence. "When Janice and I were little, our mother told us our father was dead." Lily remembered the photo of her parents supposedly taken on their honeymoon, and the faded picture of the four of them at the beach one summer afternoon.

"I didn't learn the truth until I was fourteen. It turned out that my dead father was actually alive and well. He lived twenty miles away from us in a two-story brick house with his *real* family, his wife and college-age son, and he wanted nothing to do with my mother or Janice and me. A few years ago his wife died. You'd think with her gone, he might want to get to know us, but he hasn't tried to contact either of us. Neither has his son. But I really don't care." Lily raised her head high to prove it. "He's the one losing out."

"Did he at least pay child support?"

Lily had asked her mother that question more than once. "I've never been able to find that out, but if he did, it wasn't much. We never had enough money." Her whole childhood had been spent moving from apartment to apartment, and once or twice when her mother couldn't make the rent, sleeping in the car.

"Bastard." Carter's indignation was a nice change from his anger. "Your mother probably didn't tell you because she wanted to protect you."

"No, she was protecting herself. She enjoyed her role as a young widow, and didn't want anyone to know she was actually an unwed mother. She never intended to tell us. I only found out when my grandmother was dying. Grandma said it was time we knew the truth. My mother was furious." The deception had deeply wounded Lily, and still did. "That was when I realized she lied whenever it suited her. She still does. Janice is a lot like her." Lily found a clean towel and dried her hands. "I'm the only honest one in the family."

Carter stared at her as if he'd never seen her before. What had she expected? He probably couldn't imagine having mother and sister like hers.

She attempted a laugh, but the sound that came out was lonely and sad. "Not a pretty story, is it?"

"No, and it sucks." Compassion burned in his eyes as

he took the towel from her and set it aside. He tucked her hair behind her ears with a gentle touch. "That's been bothering me all night."

His index finger caressed her cheek and she almost swooned. Holding his gaze, hardly aware of her actions, she leaned toward him.

His eyes darkened and warmed. "You're something special," he murmured.

Between his words and his intent gaze, it was difficult to think. "I am?" Lily managed to squeak. "I've been thinking the same thing about you."

"Yeah?" He traced a lazy path across her lower lip with his thumb.

Her lips parted with a sigh and she *had* to sink against him. Kiss him. In the welcoming circle of his arms she raised her face to his.

Hailey let out a wail.

Carter jerked back and so did Lily.

"Lily? I think Hailey wants you, so here she is," Henri said, dangerously close to the kitchen.

They both got busy, Carter wiping down the counter and Lily hanging up the hand towel.

She glanced at the round wall clock, surprised to see how late it was. "It's past her bedtime. I should take her home."

Henri looked from Carter to Lily and back, her sly smile unnerving.

Did she know what had almost happened? Lily hoped not. As much as she liked Henri, some things were private. Out of the corner of her eye she noted Carter's carefully blank expression and knew he shared her thoughts.

"Thanks again for a wonderful meal," she told Henri. "I'll bring Hailey back after breakfast in the morning."

Five minutes later, the baby buckled into her car seat, Lily drove home, her thoughts on the man of her dreams. Because Carter Boyle was just that. Call her impulsive— a trait that often got her into trouble. After all, she really didn't know him that well. But she knew enough. Besides, she couldn't fight what she felt in her heart—that this could be the start of something wonderful.

She could hardly wait to see him on Tuesday.

## Chapter Five

Carter was at his desk on Tuesday, sipping his morning coffee, when Linda buzzed. "Your mother's on line one."

She *would* call now, with Lily due to arrive anytime. An appointment he looked forward to way more than he should. He was still thinking about that almost-kiss and still mad at himself for going there with a client. In his mother's kitchen, no less. Talk about dangerous. But when Lily had looked at him with that soft light in her eyes, her mouth begging for attention...

His body stirred. Carter shifted in his chair. No more of that. "Put her through, and buzz me after five minutes," he said.

That'd keep the conversation nice and short.

"Hey, Mom. What's up?"

"Beautiful day, isn't it?"

He glanced out the window. No sign of clouds today. Warm, sunny weather had arrived at last. "Sure is."

"You busy?"

"Yeah." Pushing a button on his computer, he called up Lily's file and his notes and questions, then printed everything.

"I'll make this quick. I know Lily'll be there soon, and I can't reach her on her cell. Something amazing just happened, and I'm sure she'll want to know. Hailey just pulled herself up."

His mom sounded more excited than she had in a long time. Carter knew she expected him to say something. "Uh, that's great."

"Great? It's amazing. She's only seven months old, Carter, not even crawling yet. You didn't pull yourself up until you were nine months old. By that age, she'll probably be walking."

Already his mother cared about the little girl. Lily was right, she needed a grandchild. Dammit, she *had* one. If they could just find her…

"Her mother will be picking her up soon," he warned. "Don't get too attached."

"I can't help it. She's such an adorable baby."

Carter pictured the little girl's toothless grin and chubby cheeks. "She's a charmer, all right."

His mom would miss the baby after she left, would probably be down in the dumps for months. For the millionth time he wished his own daughter were part of their lives. It'd been seven years since they'd stopped looking for her. Maybe it was time to try again.

But Carter had his doubts about putting his mother or himself through the anxious wait, the awful ups and downs. And this was not the time to think about that.

"…and her aunt Lily!" his mother was saying. "She's a doll, too, don't you think?"

Talk about obvious. Carter thought Lily was hot, but he wasn't about to share that with his mother. "Knock it off, Mom."

She sniffed. "I have no idea what you're talking about."

"Right, and I'm king of the world. You made your feelings clear at dinner the other night."

"You know you enjoyed yourself. You're looking for a wife. You said so."

Cursing himself for not keeping his mouth shut, Carter shook his head. "That's beside the point."

"Admit it, son, you—"

To his relief, Linda buzzed the intercom, a loud noise that cut his mother off. *Thank you, Linda.* "I should go," Carter said.

"All right, but be sure and tell Lily to call me. Hailey's milestone is a big deal, and I want to share the joy."

Carter disconnected and punched the intercom. "Thanks for buzzing me, Linda. You're a lifesaver."

"Remember that when it comes time for my raise. Lily Gleason arrived a few minutes ago. She's delightful. She didn't want to be late, and is on her way back."

He'd barely straightened his tie before she walked in. He stood. "Hello, Lily."

"Hi," she said almost shyly.

Why that touched him, he didn't know. But it did. As she headed toward the desk he noted the short-sleeved purple shift that hugged her in all the right places. The large, pink zipper down the front was intriguing as hell. Today her legs were bare—*nice*—and she wore sandals with thin purple straps. And a delicate silver ankle bracelet. *Have mercy.* Carter cleared his throat. "You're right on time."

"I am, aren't I." Looking pleased, she flopped into the chair across his desk. "I owe that to your mother, for watching Hailey."

"She just called here, looking for you. She wants you to call her. Hailey pulled herself up this morning."

"Really? How exciting. I just wish Janice were here to see that." Lily's smile dimmed. She adjusted the dozen or so bracelets on her arm, then toyed with one long beaded earring.

Gestures Carter already recognized. She fiddled like that when something bothered her. "You're upset about your sister," he guessed.

Lily nodded. "I haven't heard from her in over a week. I must've phoned her a dozen times—in the morning, late afternoon and once after midnight. Every time, I left a message for her to call."

"Maybe her phone isn't working."

"I thought of that, but somehow I don't think that's the problem. I'm sure everyone in the band has a phone. She could borrow theirs to check in."

"Think something happened to her?"

"What I think is, she's all wrapped up in her boyfriend and singing with his band." Lily blew the usual stubborn locks of hair out of her eyes. "Tourist season starts May seventeenth. If she doesn't come back by then, I don't know what I'll do."

He was so distracted by her deep wide eyes and the strong urge to tangle his fingers in that soft, curly hair that he barely registered her comment. *Focus, Boyle.*

He reached for his pen beside Lily's folder. "That's more than a week from now. It's too soon to worry."

"You don't know my sister."

"No, but I do know my mother. Watching Hailey makes her happy. She'd probably jump at the chance to keep doing it."

"Not seven days a week. I work long hours, Carter—weekdays from 9:00 a.m. until 7:00 p.m. Cindy, one of the women who works for me, closes up at ten, but only during the week. I'm trying to hire a high school or college kid to close weekends, but if I can't, I'll be working Saturdays and Sundays till ten. That means I won't be able to pick up Hailey until ten-thirty. Then, less than twelve hours later, I'll be bringing her back again." Lily shook her head. "I couldn't do that to your mother, and I *hate* doing it to Hailey."

"No, but you could ask. Your long summer hours are like mine during tax season."

"Then you know that even with evenings off there's hardly a moment to take care of myself, let alone a baby. Hailey deserves better. She needs her mommy."

Carter liked the fact Lily cared so much about her niece, and hated the glum look on her face. She was honest and open and charming, and he'd never met anyone like her. "Janice will come get Hailey eventually," he said, wishing he could shake some sense into the woman. "I'm betting she'll call soon, too."

"She'd better." Lily glanced at his table clock and her eyes widened. "Gosh, look at the time. I have a ton of work to do, and I'm sure you do, too. You wanted to see my booth. Shouldn't we get started?"

She was right. But talking about her sister, he'd momentarily forgotten. Truth was, even if Lily had never mentioned Janice, just sitting across the desk from her was distracting as hell. How did she do that?

Carter opened her folder and glanced at the notes he'd printed out. "Before we leave, I have a few questions."

"Ask away."

The first few, about her employees and repairs to the

interior of the booth, were easy. There were several relating to inventory tracking that Lily couldn't answer right away. She promised to get back to him.

"There's one last question." Carter flipped through the tax return the IRS was auditing until he found Schedule C, the form used for self-employment income. He slid it toward Lily. "I couldn't find any backup for this carpentry expense." With his pen he pointed to the line in question.

"I paid *that* much for carpentry? Yikes. Let me think." Brow wrinkled, she stared upward.

Which gave Carter a fine view of her slender neck. The neckline of her dress curved just beneath the hollow of her throat. Below that, so close he could reach out and grab it, was the zipper tab. He imagined tugging it down. All the way down. Pictured a lacy black see-through bra and bikini panties underneath.

Stifling a groan of desire, he grasped the tax form with both hands. "Well?" he said, his voice sounding harsh and strained to his own ears.

Her eyes widened. "It was three years ago. You'd think I'd remember something that significant, but at the moment, I can't."

"It's important."

Rubbing her forehead, Lily moaned. "I knew I shouldn't have let Daryl help me that year."

"Daryl?"

"My boyfriend at the time. He said he knew about taxes, and since I don't enjoy filling out the forms, I let him do it."

"You didn't question the numbers?"

"No. I foolishly trusted him. Not too smart, huh?" She glanced down as if embarrassed. "If I'd known about you then, I wouldn't be in this fix. From now on, I'd like you to handle my taxes."

If the audit went well. If not, she'd no doubt change her mind. "Let's get through this first," he counseled.

"Are you worried that things will go badly?"

She caught her perfect lip in her teeth, and his body went haywire. The woman was killing him and didn't even realize.

"You never know," he said. "If we get a nitpicky auditor… I'll try to find out who's assigned to us. At any rate, we should be fully prepared. That means being able to back up every number on this form."

"Okay. I appreciate your honesty, Carter, and I know you'll do your best for me. Somehow I'll get you the information you need."

She smiled at him, and he felt as if he could conquer the world. "Thanks. Ready to show me your booth?"

"I'LL BE BACK IN AN HOUR," Carter told Linda as he and Lily entered the reception area.

His secretary, a smartly dressed brunette, nodded.

"Goodbye, Linda," Lily said. "I'll drop by with those earrings later in the week. You want the emerald-green beads, your favorite color, right?"

Linda nodded. "I'll have a check ready."

The woman had worked for Carter since he'd opened an office here and *he* hadn't known she liked green until now. But Lily did. "I didn't realize you and Linda knew each other," he said as they neared the glass-and-chrome door.

"We didn't until my first appointment, last week. I was early today, so we had a chance to talk. She's a sweetheart."

Carter had never thought of his fiftysomething secretary as a sweetheart. Reliable, efficient and great at her job, yes. "How do you do that?" he asked.

"Do what?"

"Make friends so easily."

"I never thought about it. Habit, I guess. A friendly personality brings in sales and repeat business."

She continued to amaze him. He held the door for her and she moved through it, her lilac scent teasing his senses. Wishing he'd brought his shades, Carter squinted as he and Lily reached the parking lot. In the bright morning sunlight her hair shone like burnished copper. The usual wayward strands flirted with her eyes. Carter balled up his fists to keep from pushing them back. He knew better than to touch her again.

"Are we walking or driving?" Lily asked.

The booths were about a mile down the road, but time was short. "I thought we'd drive to save time. Mine is that black sedan over there," he said, nodding at his car.

"So it *was* your Lexus in front of your mom's the other night. Wow. I've never ridden in one before."

Impressing her was easy and enjoyable. "It's a smooth ride," Carter said. "You'll like it."

Within seconds they were rolling out of the parking lot. As he pulled onto Main and headed toward Front Street, Lily pointed to a well-maintained, one-story brick building. "That's the place I'm buying—depending on how the audit goes." Her smile didn't quite work.

He longed to reassure her with a touch, but settled for words. "Don't court trouble."

"Think positive—I like that. Okay, I will." Lily's back straightened. "You're right about the car. It really is smooth."

Front Street was a block away. As Carter signaled and slowed to turn, he glanced at Lily. At the long stretch of thigh revealed by her short skirt. The question that had been on his mind for days slipped out. "How come a warm, sexy woman like you doesn't have a boyfriend?"

"Me, warm and sexy? Thank you." A blush colored her cheeks. "I had one but he was married. I can't believe I didn't figure that out. He was forever canceling dates at the last minute. But he said he wanted to marry me, and I loved him. So I accepted his excuses." She made the noise he'd heard the other night, the one that sounded like a laugh gone wrong. "You must think I'm a gullible fool. Well, I was."

First her parents, then this jerk. Lily had been hurt more than a few times. Carter wanted to strangle every person who'd broken her heart. Yet she was the most upbeat person he knew. "Hey," he said. "We all make mistakes."

"I'll bet you don't."

Those guileless, caramel-brown eyes met his. He wanted to be as good as she believed he was. She'd shared her past so freely, hiding nothing.

"Oh, I've made my share of mistakes," he said.

As he eased the Lexus into a parking space, he considered telling her about the daughter he'd fathered but didn't know. Except he couldn't work out a way to explain, not without stirring up questions he couldn't answer. Such as why Darla, the mother of his child, had run away and didn't want to be found. Lily was sure to pity him, and he couldn't handle that. No, the past was best kept that way—dead and buried.

"Nothing like mine, I'll bet," she said. "From now on I'm going to be more careful about who I get involved with. If a man isn't honest, I'm not interested."

"Guys will say anything to get into a woman's…to get a woman to like them." Carter set the brake and turned off the car. "You can't possibly know if they're being straight with you."

"Oh, but I can. For one thing, I'm wiser now. Besides, if you *really* pay attention to a person, you can tell. Take you. I know in here—" she pointed to her heart "—that you're one-hundred-percent honest."

Reaching across the space between the bucket seats, she touched his face.

Her eyes sought and held his and he got lost in them. His body tensed and stirred, and he knew he should pull away.

Instead he leaned toward her. "Then you must know I want to kiss you."

CARTER WAS KISSING HER. *At last.* Lily sighed and closed her eyes. His lips flirted with hers, a light, teasing brush that wasn't nearly enough. Hungry for more, she arched toward him, wrapped her arms around his neck and pulled him closer. His mouth got serious. Very serious, slanting against hers, with the promise of more to come.

A delicious warmth started in her belly and spread through her body. Heady with his spicy scent and the feel of his fingers cupping the back of her head, she melted.

When he urged her lips apart she willingly opened them. His tongue touched hers and retreated, touched again, a dance as intimate as sex. She copied his moves, tangling and delving. A groan rumbled in his chest.

He shifted back, tugging her across the space between their seats. Suddenly she was damp between her legs. Wanting, needing to be much closer, she tried to straddle his lap. A horn blared rudely.

Her eyelids jerked open. She was pressed against the steering wheel. Realizing *she* was the one honking the horn, she laughed and slipped back to her own seat. "Oops."

On the sidewalk nearby, several pedestrians glanced at them with curious interest. Lily was too dazed to care.

Beside her, Carter was breathing hard. So was she, and her heart was pounding.

"That shouldn't have happened," he said, his eyes still bright with desire. "Sometimes…" He shook his head. "It's hard to think straight around you."

"I have the same problem." She touched her still-tingly lips. "You're a good kisser." Maybe the best kisser ever.

"I liked it, too." He scrubbed his hand over his face. "I like you, Lily. But you're a client."

How she admired his honesty. It made her care even more for him. "If you're worried I'll think less of you for what just happened, don't be. It doesn't bother me at all." Except that she wanted him to do it again.

"Well, it bothers me. I'm a professional, and kissing you isn't right. Until we get through the audit, our relationship should be strictly accountant and client."

"Okay," Lily said, wondering how she'd ever keep her hands off him. Especially having experienced the warm strength of his arms around her and the avid attention of his lips.

"But when it's over, I'd like to take you out."

Lily wanted that, too. She hadn't had sex in a year, hadn't been interested. With a few kisses, Carter had awakened a powerful physical longing. She wanted him sexually, wanted to get serious and someday make babies with him. With any luck he was thinking along the same lines. Or would be in the near future. Mentally, she crossed her fingers.

He was asking her to wait approximately six more weeks. As intense as her feelings for him were, she wondered if she could do it. Then again, she'd waited a very long time for a man like Carter Boyle.

What were a mere six weeks?

"It's a date." She started to touch his shoulder, then remembered and pulled her hand back. "Come on, I'll show you my booth."

CARTER RARELY VISITED the two dozen artisan booths where tourists flocked and freely spent their money. He'd never been here before the start of tourist season. As he and Lily ambled across the packed dirt toward the neat kiosklike huts, male and female voices carried toward them, along with an oldies song from someone's radio. The air radiated with warmth and camaraderie.

Everyone seemed to know Lily. People waved and called out greetings, which she returned. Many eyed Carter, especially the men.

He wanted to put his arm around Lily and let them know she was taken, but didn't. Until the audit ended he had no claim on her. A glare or two couldn't hurt, though.

"You know all these people?" he asked, narrowing his eyes at a lanky young male wearing a do-rag, who regarded Lily with a definitely sexual expression.

Which she seemed oblivious to. "Every one. We're all here so much during the season that we get pretty close."

"How close?" he asked, knowing he sounded possessive.

"If a shoplifter comes around we let each other know. If we need a break we watch each other's booths—stuff like that." She gave him a sideways look. "You're the only man who interests me, Carter."

God, that felt good. And a little scary. Things were moving too fast. "Whoa," he said. "You may be the first client I've ever asked out, but we're not even dating yet."

"I shouldn't have said that, huh. I only meant that I like you and think you're a great guy. That's all."

She gave a friendly smile and stared into his eyes and Carter believed her. He relaxed.

"Hi, Lily!" An attractive brunette hurried toward her. "I haven't seen you in days." She glanced curiously at Carter. "Who's this?"

"Meet Carter Boyle, my accountant. Carter, this is my best friend, Charity Lindemeyer. She makes the prettiest wind socks and coolest chimes you'll ever see."

"I'll custom-craft any design you want."

"I'll keep that in mind. Pleasure." Carter offered his hand.

"Yes, it is." Charity shook and offered a broad smile. "I've heard *so* much about you."

Lily muttered something unintelligible, and Carter wondered what she'd told her friend. He'd only kissed her a few minutes ago, so it couldn't have been much. Curious, he raised his eyebrows. "Like what?"

"Nothing at all," Lily said. "Carter needs to see my booth to prepare for the audit, and we don't have much time, so we'd better get going."

"Okay, but we haven't talked in a while," Charity said. "I miss you. There's so much to catch up on. For starters, I have a date for lunch today with Trevor." Happiness radiated from her. "Hey, we're not meeting for half an hour. If you two want, you could join us when you're through here."

"Um, we can't," Lily said. "We'll probably be a while."

"Some other time, then. I'll call you tonight, Lily."

When Charity disappeared, Lily blew out a breath. "That was so embarrassing."

"She's almost as bad as my mom." Hands low on his hips, Carter shook his head. "What exactly did you tell her about me?"

"Only that Henri's taking care of Hailey and that you and I had dinner at her house on Sunday. I'll explain about us not dating till after the audit, so she'll quit with the looks and comments. My booth is over there."

As Carter headed toward it with Lily, he wondered what she'd tell Charity now. Would she mention those hot kisses? *Hot* being the operative word here. Lily Gleason tasted even better than she looked. Carter had sensed the passion simmering inside her. He wanted to unleash it, watch her come apart as he pleasured her. A certain part of him began to wake up. He silently swore. Waiting wouldn't be easy.

"This is it," Lily said.

A metal curtain covered the open space above the counter. Key in hand, Lily moved to the door. As she bent to unlock it, her skirt inched up. Carter studied the backs of her thighs. Would they feel as smooth as they looked?

"Sometimes it sticks," she said over her shoulder.

He jerked his gaze up. "Need help?"

"No, I'll get it."

She focused on the door, and he went back to scoping her out. From what he could see, she had one sweet little behind. He itched to fit his palms to it and—

With a silent oath he cut off his thoughts. If he kept that up, he'd never be able to keep his hands off her until June nineteenth.

"Got it," she said, pushing the door open and gesturing him inside. "Welcome to my home away from home."

The small space was barely big enough for both of them, and with the metal curtain down, the muffled sounds outside and scant light from the door, the booth felt intimate. Carter smelled fresh paint and Lily's lilac scent. He fantasized lifting her onto the narrow counter, her thighs gripping his hips and her face flushed with pleasure. Now he had a hard-on.

Luckily, Lily's gaze was trained on the ceiling. "Maybe I should've painted the ceiling white. Do you think there's too much purple in here?"

"Not at all," Carter said. "The color suits you." He nodded at the metal shade. "I'll bet that really cuts down on break-ins. This is a great setup."

"The space is too small, but it works. We got the shades last year, and thank goodness. I was so tired of locking everything in the van at night, then arranging the displays again in the morning—what a pain. Now I just lock up and go."

At the courthouse a few blocks away, eleven o'clock chimed in the clock tower. Their meeting had started over an hour ago. It felt like much less. They both had work to do.

"That's all I need for now," Carter said. "We should go."

"If you have more questions, just ask," Lily said as they strolled toward the car.

"I'm sure I will." From now on, he'd call her instead of meeting in person. Safer that way.

They drove back to the office in comfortable silence. Until Lily turned in her seat to look at him.

"Carter? Do you ever think about having kids?"

The question hit like a punch to the gut.

Carter worked to keep his expression neutral. He had no idea how to answer that. Tell her he already had a daughter but didn't know her name or where she lived? Uh-uh, not going there. "Do you?" he asked, stalling for time.

She nodded. "A houseful. When I was little, I always wished I had more brothers and sisters—a big, happy family."

Instead she'd been stuck with a mother who lied, a father who wanted nothing to do with her, and a self-centered sister. Didn't that suck.

"I wanted that, too," he admitted. "But it was just me and my parents."

"They didn't want any more kids?"

"They talked about giving me a brother or sister, but it never happened."

"That explains it."

"Explains what?"

"Sometimes when your mom holds Hailey, she gets a sad look on her face. She's wishing she'd had more kids."

Lily was mistaken about the reason for his mother's sorrow, but Carter wasn't about to correct her.

"Maybe. But for me, aside from loneliness, being an only child wasn't a bad deal. I got all the attention. If I wanted to ski, my parents took lessons with me. When I wanted to be an astronaut, they sent me to space camp." He shook his head, remembering how they'd saved up to send him to the expensive camp. "They spoiled me rotten."

"You're not spoiled. If you were, you wouldn't be so good to your mom. Spending every Sunday night with her—that's really sweet."

His ears burned and he knew he was blushing. "Well, she is the only mother I have." Even if she did butt into his business.

He thought again about Lily's question. The other night

he'd pictured two kids in his house. Now he imagined four. Laughing at the kitchen table. Running down the hallways. Playing and fighting the way it'd been with some of his friends and their siblings. "I definitely want kids," he said.

"I knew it."

A tiny smile played at her lips, making him wonder what she was thinking.

"You'll make a wonderful father, Carter."

"Thanks," he said, knowing she'd change her story if she heard about the daughter he'd never met. What kind of father was that? A lousy one.

For the rest of the drive back, that burned in his gut. Yet he managed to keep up his end of the conversation—more or less.

"Is everything okay?" Lily asked as he pulled into the parking lot of his building. "You seem…I don't know. Different."

"Just thinking about my two o'clock." He forced a smile. "Everything's fine."

## Chapter Six

At two-thirty Wednesday, missing Hailey and in need of an afternoon off, Lily knocked on Henri's door.

The older woman opened it wearing a bib apron and a smudge of flour on her nose. "Lily," she said, smiling. "I didn't expect you for a few more hours. Come in."

Lily wiped her feet and stepped inside. "I know I'm early, but I thought I'd spend the rest of the afternoon with Hailey." Every day she loved the little girl more. When Janice took her back to Seattle next week, she'd take a piece of Lily's heart, too. And leave a gaping hole in her life. Which was why she was eager to play with her niece now.

Standing in the small entry, she glanced at the living room. She didn't see Hailey or hear any baby sounds. "Where is she?"

"We had a busy morning," Henri said. "She *just* fell asleep."

Knowing Hailey, she'd sleep for a good two hours. Lily had so looked forward to spending this time together. "I'd better not wake her," she said, disappointed. "Looks as if you're busy in the kitchen. Guess I'll work a few more hours, after all, and come back later."

"Don't be silly," Henri said. "I'm just starting to mix up a batch of snickerdoodles and could use some help." She beckoned Lily closer, as if to share a secret, and lowered her voice. "They're Carter's favorites."

Since Lily wanted to know everything about him, she was pleased to learn this. Even if she didn't know how to cook. "I'd like to help, but I'd probably burn them."

"The other night you said you wanted to learn to cook. This is the perfect time to start."

"A cooking lesson." Why not? If things worked out with Carter—*slow down, Lily,* she sternly reminded herself, but couldn't help imagining they would—she'd be able to bake his favorite cookies anytime. "That'd be great."

"Then wash up, grab an apron from the bottom drawer and let's get started."

Ten minutes later, Lily was creaming butter, shortening and sugar with an electric mixer.

"You want the butter soft for these cookies," Henri said from the kitchen table, where she sat nursing a cup of peppermint tea. "But if you're making piecrust, it should be ice-cold, straight from the refrigerator. Now, as you slowly add the flour mixture, keep the mixer on low speed. That way the flour doesn't spatter all over."

She was full of good advice. "I should be taking notes," Lily said. "So I don't forget anything."

"You can do that while the dough chills. Once everything is good and mixed, you're going to wrap it in wax paper and put it in the fridge for an hour."

Lily set the dough in the refrigerator. "I'm ready for more tea," Henri said. "Would you like some while you jot down those baking notes?"

"That'd be nice."

"I'll pour the water, you get yourself a pen and paper. They're in that drawer under the phone."

Henri's catch-all drawer was neatly organized, not at all like the mishmash in Lily's. Once tourist season ended and she bought Mr. Creech's building—with Carter in charge of the audit she *knew* it would happen—she'd straighten up that drawer and the rest of her house, too.

In no time she'd scribbled down Henri's tips. As she sipped her tea she heard the ring of her cell phone, which was in her purse in the living room.

This close to tourist season, it could be important. "I'd better see who that is." She hurried to answer. "Hello?"

"It's Janice."

*About time.* Stifling the urge to lecture her sister, Lily sank onto the sofa and forced herself to remain calm. "Where have you been?" she asked, pleased that she sounded curious instead of angry.

"I don't have to answer to you."

Oops. Some of her frustration must've showed after all. "Actually, since I have your daughter, you do."

After a tense pause, Janice huffed out a loud breath. "It's not like I'm dodging you, Lily. I'm working, singing my heart out. It's paying off, too. People love us! That's why I called. The tour's been extended through the end of May."

No wonder Janice was so touchy. She wouldn't be back on time. Lily had suspected as much. Although she loved having Hailey, this was not good news. "But you promised," she said. "You know my busy season starts next week."

"I can't lose this opportunity."

"But Hailey's your daughter. She needs you."

"I've made up my mind, Lily. I'm doing this." Stubbornness rang in every word.

"You haven't even asked about her. Don't you miss her?" *Don't you care?*

"Sure I do. How's she doing?"

"Yesterday she pulled herself up. Pretty soon she'll be moving all over, and it'll be harder to keep her away from my beading supplies."

"So that's what this is about. Just pile them on the counters where she can't reach."

"You've seen my counters. They're already crammed with stuff. There's not enough room for everything."

"I'm sure you'll think of something. You always do."

Lily heard a masculine voice in the background, and Janice's muffled reply. She must've covered the mouthpiece.

"We're about to rehearse a new song. I have to go. Thanks, Lily. I owe you."

"Two extra weeks and that's *it*," Lily said.

But Janice was gone.

What to do now? Shaking her head, Lily trudged back to the kitchen.

Still seated at the table, Henri frowned. "Goodness, that's a long face. I hope you didn't get bad news."

"That was Janice—Hailey's mother—on the phone. She's not coming back next week."

"When will she be back, and where is she?"

"Somewhere in the Midwest, singing with her boy-friend's band. Their tour just got extended and now she's saying she'll be here at the end of the month. She didn't even ask about Hailey until I pushed her to. I'm starting to doubt she even cares."

"That's sad."

And worrisome. Hailey deserved better. "It's not that I don't love and enjoy my niece. I do. But once tourist season starts next week, I'll be working ten hours a day, seven days a week. What am I going to do with her?"

Henri gave her an isn't-it-obvious look. "Let me go on taking care of her, of course."

Carter had said his mother wouldn't mind, but still… "I can't ask you to do that, Henri. It's too much."

"I'll be the judge of that. She takes a good two-hour nap, so it's not that tiring."

"But—"

Henri silenced her with a gesture. "Just listen. If I get worn-out or need to go someplace without her, I know several women, all longing for grandchildren, who'd love to help out. Hailey's such a joy. Her noises, her laugh, her funny antics—they fill my heart."

Her eyes were sad again. After what Carter had said yesterday, Lily knew why—she was wishing she'd had more children.

With that Lily made up her mind. Hailey adored Henri, and vice versa. The baby brought Henri joy, and Lily couldn't deprive the woman her surrogate grandchild.

She was so grateful that she leaned down and hugged her. "Thanks, Henri. I don't know how I'll ever repay you. How about a raise?"

When the hug ended, Henri was beaming. "Forget the raise. Your friendship and Hailey's company are payment enough. Now, it's just about time to take the dough out of the fridge and make little balls to roll in cinnamon sugar…."

LATER THAT EVENING, after playing with Hailey for a while and tucking her in for the night, Lily was still smiling. With Henri offering to continue babysitting, and Hailey so good-natured, it was impossible not to feel happy. Lily cleared off a space on the coffee table and laid out her tools, wire and the emerald crystal beads. It was time to finish the earrings Linda had ordered.

She called Charity and put her on speakerphone. "You'll never guess what I did this afternoon," Lily said.

"It must be something besides work, or you wouldn't be asking me to guess. I know, you made out with Carter Boyle. Who, by the way, is yummy."

"Isn't he? I wish. But I didn't even see him today." Lily hoped to in the morning, when she delivered Linda's earrings.

"In that case, hmm… You bought a new outfit for when Carter takes you out. Has he asked you yet? Because the way he looked at you yesterday, he's interested."

Remembering those bone-melting kisses, Lily had to agree. "We talked about dating, but he doesn't think it's right to go out until after the audit."

"Well, shoot. So that means no new outfit?"

"Nope."

"Then I'm all out of guesses. What *did* you do this afternoon?"

"Made snickerdoodles."

"Get out! You can't bake."

"I know." Lily laughed. "Henri's teaching me. I made them in her kitchen, with her help. They turned out pretty well. I should know. She gave me some to take home and they're half-gone."

"Wow, you and Henri are getting tight."

"She's the best, especially after Janice's latest." Lily updated Charity. "Without Henri's help, I don't know what I'd do."

"I know what I'd like to do—smack your sister. What *is* she thinking?"

"Not about Hailey, that's for sure." Lily didn't want to discuss her sister anymore, which would ruin what was left of her good mood. "How was your lunch yesterday with Trevor?"

"Wonderful. We're going out again Saturday night, to the Gull's Nest. We both love that pub, and some new band is playing there, so we'll get to dance together. Keep your fingers crossed they play some slow songs. But if they don't we just might pretend."

Lily grinned. "You don't like Trevor much, do you?"

"I'm wild about him. And pretty sure he feels the same way about me."

Her friend sounded joyful. A week ago Lily would've been jealous. Now, with her own romance on the verge of blossoming, she was thrilled for Charity. "That's so great."

"It is. Hey, you should mention the Gull's Nest to your sister. Maybe the band she sings with will get a gig there. Then she'll have to take Hailey."

"Good idea." The phone clicked, signaling another call. "There's my other line. Be right back…. Hello?" Lily said.

"It's Carter."

His deep voice vibrated through her, and her insides fluttered. "Hi. I'm on the other line. Hold on while I get off." Slightly breathless, she returned to Charity. "It's Carter."

"Ooh. Call me later."

"Hi, again," Lily said, setting down the earring she'd nearly finished. Hugging herself like a lovesick teen, she nestled into the corner of the love seat. "What's up?"

"I found out who's doing your audit."

He'd called to tell her this at nine o'clock at night?

"Aha." Lily swallowed her disappointment. Was this how it was going to be for the next six weeks—make that five weeks and five days? Well, he'd warned her. And this was a good reminder to slow down. "And?" she asked.

"It's not good. His name is Michael Woods, and he's audited several of my clients. He's a real stickler."

Bleak news that made Lily feel queasy. "You're scaring me. I'll probably have nightmares tonight."

"Don't do that. At least we know who we're dealing with. We'll go in superprepared. Trust me, it'll be okay."

He sounded so confident. She believed him. "I do trust you. And I just remembered what that carpentry expense was for. That was the year Daryl, the guy who did my taxes, built me a worktable."

"For that price?" Carter whistled. "Must be some table."

"It is," Lily said. "But I don't remember it costing as much as my tax return says." Why hadn't she paid closer attention to what Daryl did? Because she'd trusted him. Foolish! An unpleasant thought occurred to her. "Oh, dear, what if he padded the cost to lower my taxes?"

"Then we have a problem. Can you find the invoice?"

"I kept all my receipts in that grocery bag you have. If he gave me one, it'd be in there."

"I've been through everything in that bag. There's no sign of it."

Things just kept getting worse. *Trust me,* Carter had said. But not even *he* could fix this. Lily sighed. "What'll I do now?"

"If you still have the table, measure the height, width and length and take pictures. Once you have the dimensions, it won't be hard to price the materials in today's dollars. I have a computer program that will calculate what they cost three years ago. You'll also want to get in touch with a carpenter or two and find out what they'd charge to make something comparable."

Lily was impressed with this solution. "What a smart idea. I kept the table for a few months, but it was too big for my little houseboat. So I gave it to Joyce, the single mom who works for me. It's in her basement. We're actually having a meeting at her house tomorrow morning." Their last before tourist season started. "I'll measure it then. After I research the materials and talk to a contractor I'll get back to you."

"Excellent."

Lily thought so, too—since that meant talking to Carter again soon. She picked up the almost-finished earring and reached for her flat-nose pliers. "It's late. Why are you still at the office?"

"Actually, I'm at home."

"You didn't have to call tonight." Not to discuss business.

"I wanted to."

The low timbre of his voice hummed through her. This was more like it. She imagined his expression, dark and intent, and her heart almost burst through her chest. Suddenly feeling a whole lot better, she squeezed a crimp into place, securing the dangling beads. "Have you talked to your mom this evening?"

"No. Why?"

*She taught me how to make your favorite cookies.* Lily decided to keep that to herself—for now. She recalled the look on Carter's face when Henri had offered her cooking lessons, and hoped he wouldn't be upset. Or think she was moving too fast, or that Henri was—

"Lily? Are you there?"

"Sorry. Janice finally called. I was right, she won't be here next week. She'll be gone till the end of the month."

"Bummer."

"Yeah." The only good part about it was keeping Hailey in her life a while longer. Lily held up the finished earring, admiring the way the lamplight glinted off the beads. "You were right—your mom still wants to take care of Hailey. I think ten-plus hours a day, seven days a week, is way too much, but she claims that several friends will help if she needs them." Lily frowned. "Do you think I should look for someone else? Just in case it's too much?"

"She wouldn't do it if she didn't want to, but finding a backup isn't a bad idea."

"I'll ask around, then." Lily punched her finished creation through a specially designed earring card, beside its mate. The beads clinked softly.

"You're working right now," Carter said.

"I just finished Linda's earrings. They turned out really well, and I think she'll be pleased." The card fit nicely in the small cardboard Designs by Lily jewelry box. "I thought I'd stop by your office in the morning and give them to her." Anticipating a warm response, she caught her breath.

"Linda will like that," he said. "But I won't be in—I have a meeting at Island Air."

His tone wasn't exactly cold, but neither was it warm and intimate. He sounded like her accountant, nothing more. Even though he'd warned her it would be this way until the audit was over, she couldn't help feeling let down. At the very least she wanted Carter to ask her to come later, when he'd be there. *Anything* that hinted at the budding romance she'd been so certain of yesterday.

But he didn't.

Seconds later, they hung up. Lily stared thoughtfully at her hands. Maybe Carter didn't like her as much as she did him. Certainly he was attracted to her and had kissed her as if he meant it. And, yes, he'd said he wanted to date her after the audit. Which was great, but didn't mean he felt anything close to what she did. Every day her feelings for him grew and deepened, even when she tried to hold them back.

Lonely and a tad down in the dumps, Lily tiptoed into the bedroom to check on Hailey, who often kicked off her covers. Then she would wake up, cold and unhappy. As Lily pulled the blanket up and tenderly tucked it around her niece's little body, she inhaled Hailey's sweet baby smell. Her heart filled with love for the precious child.

How could Janice bear to stay away?

Closing her eyes, Lily silently repeated the fervent wish she'd made over her birthday candles. *Someday in the not too distant future, let me find true love and make a baby. Just like Hailey,* she added.

She tried not to imagine Carter as the father of her child, tried to squash the warmth in her heart. But it was too late for that. Already she was half in love with the man.

Yesterday she'd foolishly jumped to conclusions, believing he wanted a future with her. Now she realized that beyond a date or two, he might not.

But she wanted that future. And it scared her. Because as sure as the night was dark, she'd set herself up for heartache.

AFTER DROPPING OFF HAILEY Thursday morning, Lily met Cindy and Joyce at Joyce's house. They sat in the living room, which though small by most people's standards was almost twice the size of Lily's.

"Before we discuss business, I need to look at that work-table I gave you," Lily said. "To take measurements and figure out what kind of wood it's made of."

Joyce frowned. "I really like that table. You're not thinking of taking it back, are you?"

"Where would I put it?" Lily shook her head. "This is for the audit. When Daryl made it, he claimed it as an expense. A *huge* expense." The sick feeling in her stomach was back. "He didn't give me an invoice or any receipts, so I need measurements and photos. Then I'll price the materials, talk to a few carpenters and give the information to Carter." The man she cared for way too much. "My accountant," she explained glumly.

Her employees shared a look.

"Cindy and I will help," Joyce said. "And you can tell us what's going on with Carter."

"Because I'm thinking that sad face has nothing to do with the audit." Cindy's expression darkened with worry. "Is there something you're not telling us? Should we be looking for new jobs?"

"Don't even go there," Lily said as she followed the two women down the wood stairs to where Joyce worked. "You're right, Cindy, this is personal."

They entered the daylight basement. Lily envied her the large space with its washer and dryer and big work area. If all went well with the audit and she bought Mr. Creech's building, she'd soon have an even bigger studio herself.

Tape measure in hand, she approached the worktable. With Joyce and Cindy's help, in no time she jotted down the measurements and snapped photos from several angles.

"So, what's the deal with your accountant?" Cindy asked. "What's got you feeling blue?"

"I'm falling for him." Lily tried to smile. "Can you believe that?"

"Oh, Lily." Joyce radiated sympathy. "How did that happen?"

"You know me—Miss Impulsive. He's honest and smart and a really good man, and I just can't help myself. The other day, I showed him the booth and… We kissed." Her cheeks felt hot and she knew she was blushing. "And it was wonderful."

"Wow." Joyce shook her head. "I'm jealous. It's been ages since a man kissed me."

"What's wrong with falling for him?" Cindy asked. "Unless he's married?"

"He's single," Lily assured her friends. "I made certain of that. After the audit he wants to date me. He's never dated a client before."

"It all sounds great," Joyce said as they started up the stairs. "Am I missing something?"

"The thing is, I care more than he does. I'm already hearing wedding bells, but all he wants is a date. I'm afraid of getting hurt again."

"Oh, sweetie, you *are* moving too fast." At the top of the stairs, Cindy squeezed Lily's shoulder. "Don't let him know how much you care, or you'll definitely scare him away."

"I know." Back in the living room, Lily dropped dejectedly into an armchair. "I'm thirty years old. I'm supposed to be a mature, rational woman who doesn't jump into things with both feet—at least not this quickly."

"Sometimes jumping in is a good thing," Cindy said as she settled onto the sofa. "It worked well with your jewelry business."

Joyce sat down beside her. "But not so well with men. What are you going to do?"

A question Lily had been asking herself since Carter's call last night. "Pull back. Like Cindy said, pretend I'm not that interested and that I only like him a little."

"You're not great at pretending," Joyce said.

Which was true. But if Lily set her mind to it and convinced herself that she and Carter really were client and accountant and nothing more, she could do it. "I'll give it my best try," she said. "From this moment on, I'm Carter Boyle's client, period." Brushing her hands together—easy peasy—she smiled. "Let's start our meeting."

## Chapter Seven

By the time Friday night rolled around Carter was a freaking mess, thanks to Lily's ridiculous call that afternoon. She'd phoned to give him the information on the worktable, which was great. It was her cool, stilted manner that had him shaking his head. She'd acted mad. Or maybe offended.

Which threw him. Everything had seemed fine when he'd called the other night. What had changed since then?

A quick mental search came up empty, so he'd simply asked, "You okay?"

"I'm fine—*wonderful,*" Lily had replied, her forceful tone implying the opposite.

She was upset, all right, but before he could question her she'd hung up.

Clueless, he'd asked Linda. His secretary, who loved her new dangly earrings, had only shrugged. "We chatted a bit before I put her call through. She seemed okay to me."

But she wasn't, and wondering what he'd said or done had gnawed at him ever since. Was she one of those women who expected a phone call every day?

At eight o'clock, hands stuffed into his slacks pockets, he headed up Whaler's Wharf Lane toward Houseboat

Row. This time of year, the sun didn't set until after nine. The sky was cloudless, and the deep pink sunset tinged the twilight blue. In the stillness, the darkening water glistened and gulls squawked and wheeled overhead. Normally Carter would've enjoyed the evening and the salt tang of the air, would've looked forward to getting up well before dawn tomorrow for a relaxing day of fishing with Alex.

Tonight he was too preoccupied. He eyed the brightly painted houseboats tethered to both sides of the dock. Which one was Lily's? He was about to find out.

She wasn't expecting him, and for damned sure he hadn't planned to stop by. He hadn't been home since this morning and needed to get back and lay out his fishing gear. But first he needed answers. To find out what had her acting so stiff and formal. Then he'd leave. He wouldn't even think about wanting her.

He reached the dock, his footsteps thudding on the wood. Men and women were milling around, chatting as they watered flowers or relaxed in lounge chairs. To a person they smiled or waved. Unable to work up a grin, Carter nodded. None of these house numbers matched Lily's, and he was almost halfway down the dock.

A round, elderly man walking a leashed pug was headed his way. "Evening," he said, his dog sniffing Carter's pant legs.

"Hey, pooch." Carter bent down to rub behind the animal's ears, and earned a lick for his efforts. He straightened to find the man scrutinizing him.

"Solicitations are illegal on the Row," he said.

"I'm not selling anything." Carter slid a business card from his hip pocket. "I'm Carter Boyle and I'm looking for Lily Gleason."

"Ah." After careful study of the card, the old man stroked his chin. "I'm Elliott Creech. I own a building near your office. Used to walk past it nearly every day. You a decent accountant?"

"My clients think so."

"Tell me, what are Lily's chances with the audit?"

At first the question surprised Carter, but knowing Lily, she'd probably told everyone she knew about her situation. "That's confidential," he said.

"She won't mind if you tell me. Anyway, I have the right to know. She's supposed to buy my building in the fall. I need to know if the audit will wipe out her savings."

Lily had never mentioned that the owner of the building she wanted lived in her neighborhood. Interesting. Carter understood the man's concerns. But even if he could reasonably predict the outcome of the audit, and nobody could do that, he wasn't about to share any information about a client. That was up to Lily.

"The audit isn't until the middle of June, and I have no idea what will happen," Carter said. "What I *do* know is she wants your building. I hope you're willing to wait until next month."

The man stiffened. "Course I am. Just asking, is all. She's always been so good to me, an old curmudgeon. Woman's an angel—my angel. I want her to have it." An instant later his lips twitched and he lowered his voice. "If I were forty years younger…whoo, boy."

One more person Lily had charmed. Was there a human being anywhere who didn't like her?

The pug whined and cocked its head at its master. "Okay, okay, we're going," Mr. Creech muttered. "Lily's place is near the end of the row, the one with the yellow-

and-purple wind sock, next to the place with a For Sale sign. That's mine, so if you know of anyone looking to buy a houseboat… You treat her nice, now."

The warning caught Carter off guard. He narrowed his eyes. "Why, what'd she tell you?"

"I don't know what you're talking about," Mr. Creech said. Shaking his head, he walked away.

Moments later, edgier and more confused than ever, Carter knocked on Lily's door.

"It's unlocked," she called out.

He opened it partway and peered inside. She and Hailey were on the floor in what had to be the tiniest living room ever. Kneeling in the only available space in the place, wearing faded jeans and a snug T-shirt, she was smiling and zipping up the baby's pajamas.

Carter had never seen a more beautiful woman. And he sure liked her in that shirt. "Hey," he said.

"Carter." Her eyes widened. Holding on to Hailey, she struggled to her feet. With one hand she smoothed down her shirt. "I thought you were one of the neighbors. What are you doing here?"

"I was in the neighborhood."

The baby's face lit up. Gurgling a greeting, she reached out to him. Without knowing how it happened, he was in the room and the child was in his arms. She must've just had a bath, for her face was shiny clean, her hair was damp and she smelled of talcum powder. Her chubby little fingers grasped his biceps and she pressed her head against his chest.

"She learned how to give hugs today," Lily said as she quickly cleared a space on the love seat.

"Ah." With his heart feeling as big as the sky, Carter rested his cheek on the little round head.

Lily had the sweetest expression on her face, but when she noticed him watching her, she compressed her lips and turned away.

His gut twisted. "You're mad at me." He handed Hailey to her. "If it's because I haven't called, I—"

"Don't be silly. We're both really busy. As I said on the phone this afternoon, I'm fine."

Glancing everywhere but at him, she pulled the chair from the desk in the corner and settled Hailey on her lap. Leaving him the love seat.

The Lily he knew was open and straightforward, and always looked directly at him. This new behavior wasn't like her. Carter scratched the back of his neck. "I know you too well, Lily. There definitely *is* something wrong."

"Not anything I care to discuss right now." She clasped her hands protectively around Hailey.

*Okay then.* Carter sat down. His knees touched the coffee table, which was piled with beads and tools and baby toys. He thought about nudging the thing back a few inches, but feared everything would fall off. Besides, the room was so small, there really was no place to move it.

No wonder the worktable Lily's ex had made didn't fit.

"We're a little cramped for space," she said with an apologetic look. "That's why I want that building. Once Janice picks up Hailey and I move my bead business out of here, it'll be a lot less crowded."

As crammed with stuff as it was, the place felt homey and warm—just like Lily. So different from his tidy, spacious, empty-feeling house. "I like it," he said.

"Me, too. Mainly because it's all mine."

"I met Elliott Creech on the dock. You never mentioned that he's your neighbor. He asked about the audit."

"He did? I already told him things would probably be fine." She fiddled with her earring. "What did you say?"

"That it's none of his business."

"I'll bet he didn't like that." Her lips twitched in a slight smile. "What did *he* say?"

That Carter should treat Lily nice. Which he was doing and had *been* doing. "He wants you to have his building. He really likes you." So did Carter.

"That I already know." Hailey pulled at Lily's bracelets. Murmuring softly, Lily nuzzled the crown of the baby's head.

The light was back in her eyes, and when she smiled at Carter, the world righted itself.

Without warning, Hailey squirmed and started to fuss.

"Wet diaper?" Carter asked.

"I doubt it. It's her bedtime. I should put her down for the night."

"Then we'll talk."

Lily opened her mouth, closed it.

"I'm getting up at 3:00 a.m. tomorrow to go fishing, so I won't stay long."

"Wow, that's early. All right." Once again she wouldn't meet his eyes. "How about something to drink—tea or a glass of wine?"

"Wine, thanks."

He'd only come here to find out what had upset her. He would *not* think about kissing her, or running his hands over those seductive curves…. His traitorous body stirred, and Carter knew he was in big trouble.

"If you don't mind helping yourself, the glasses are in

the cabinet to the left of the sink, and the wine is in the fridge," Lily said. "Please pour me one, too."

A glass of wine and some answers. Then he was out of here.

HAILEY'S EYELIDS DROOPED and she sucked contentedly on her pacifier. Within moments she'd fall asleep, yet Lily took her time tucking the baby in.

She needed a moment to figure out what to do. Carter didn't want to get involved, not now. And even when he did, it might just be for a date or two. For the sake of her heart, she was supposed to keep her distance. Had done it, too, for two whole days now. But she was no actress, and though she'd meant for this afternoon's phone call to be short and businesslike, she'd bungled it. Now Carter was right here, in her house, asking her what was the matter.

She had to tell him *something,* while somehow holding herself aloof. That wouldn't be easy.

It was wonderful to see him, and when he looked at her with eyes so focused and intense…

Hold herself aloof? Who was she kidding? How could she possibly resist Carter Boyle?

His being here was nothing short of dangerous. "I should send him home, don't you think?" she asked in a low voice Carter couldn't hear.

Hailey stared at her with round, trusting eyes, her cheeks flexing as she worked the pacifier.

"You're telling me to be thankful for his honesty, to be myself, and that everything will work out, aren't you?" Lily swore the baby nodded. "Okay, but I'm sticking to my desk chair like hot glue to a bracelet. Nighty night, sweetie pie."

When she returned to the living room, Carter was in the kitchen pouring wine into two glasses. The galley was so small and the man so big, there was hardly a space for Lily. Sitting on a bar stool with the counter between them seemed the way to go. Unfortunately, both stools were crammed with supplies, and so was the counter. Lily stood behind the stools.

"Is she asleep?" Carter asked.

"Not quite yet," she whispered, placing her finger over her lips.

His gaze dropped to her mouth before it jerked up again. He looked for a place to set her wine. Since there was none, he reached across the counter and stools and handed her the glass.

She tried to avoid skin-to-skin contact. He clasped the bowl of the glass, so she grasped the stem. But like magnet and iron, their fingers sought each other and met. Warmth filled her hand, then spread like fire through a parched, dry meadow.

She knew Carter felt something, too, because his eyes seemed to smolder. Then he made a strangled sound and curled his hand around hers.

Lily forgot about keeping her distance. She wished the stools and counter would magically disappear, because all she wanted was to be in Carter's arms.

He plucked the glass from her and put it someplace. Circled the counter. Then he was in front of her, pulling her into his arms.

*Home.*

With a sigh Lily snuggled against his broad chest.

"God, I've missed holding you." His breath blew hot against the shell of her ear.

Desire shivered through her, and she closed her eyes. "I know."

She wrapped her arms around him. Felt his muscles bunch and tense under her touch. His heart thundering—or was that hers?—he backed her against the refrigerator. Pinned her there with his hard body. As if he thought she'd run away.

That was the last thing she wanted to do. Smart or not, she was right where she wanted to be, and every nerve in her body was primed for his kiss. Twining her arms around his neck, she urged his head down. And waited for his mouth to claim hers.

Only nothing happened. When she blinked her eyes open, his mouth was a hairbreadth from hers.

"If you don't kiss me," she said, "I swear I'll die."

"BELIEVE ME, I'm right there with you," Carter said.

Lily's eyes were liquid with need. Her soft curves fit against him perfectly. His body felt too hard and tight for his skin, ready to explode, and his mind clouded. For one long moment the only thing that mattered was devouring Lily's mouth. But first he needed answers. With supreme effort he stepped back.

"Somehow I upset you, and so help me God, I won't kiss you until I know what I did."

Cool air filled the space between them but did nothing to bank his lust. Without asking, he cleared both bar stools, setting the supplies on the floor. Taking one chair for himself, he pushed the other a few feet away, then gestured for Lily to sit down.

She stayed where she was, her back against the refrigerator. "You didn't do anything," she said, hugging her waist. "It's me."

Of all the possible replies, Carter had never considered that one. He frowned. "I'm not following you."

Though the room was a comfortable temperature, she chafed her arms. "I've always been impulsive, especially about my feelings. And…well, you know how I value honesty. You're about the most honest man I've ever known. And a great guy, who actually listens when I talk." Blushing, she dipped her head. "Plus, I think you're very attractive."

Carter liked what she was saying. But that bit about honesty… There was a chunk of his past, a big part of who he was, that Lily knew nothing about. His conscience twinged, and he knew he should tell her about his daughter. But this wasn't the right time. He'd tell her, he assured himself. Soon.

"And that's a problem why?" he asked.

"I can't believe I'm going to say this," she mumbled, "but it's a problem because you don't like me as much as I like you. That sounds so high school." She buried her head in her hands.

Women could be so confusing. Carter crossed his arms. "Where'd you get a crazy idea like that?"

Staring at the linoleum, Lily shrugged.

They weren't getting anywhere, so he slid off the stool. "Hey." He tipped up her chin, forcing her to look at him. "Believe me, there's nothing high school about you. You're all woman. Let's go into the living room." Clasping her wrist, he tugged her toward the love seat.

He gently pushed her down, then sat beside her. On the small couch they were so close their thighs touched. The warmth of her leg against his about did him in.

He took hold of Lily's hands. "I like you. A lot. That's why I want to date you after the audit."

"But the other night, when you called to tell me about the auditor, you were so impersonal. I thought…" She pulled her hands from his and adjusted her bracelets. "That maybe you changed your mind."

"You thought wrong." Carter tucked her hair behind her ears. "I think about you all the time." His thumb stroked her smooth, soft cheek. "I'm more interested in you than I've ever been in any woman," he admitted, knowing he could be setting himself up for trouble later, if things between them didn't work out. "Do you believe me?"

"I'm not sure. Maybe you should kiss me again and convince me."

"Now that you've given me the answers I needed…" He put his arm around her shoulders and angled closer. Cupped her nape, settled his mouth on hers and tenderly showed her how he felt.

Uttering a breathy sigh, she sank against him. She tasted as sweet as before. No, better. His body stirred and hardened. He deepened the kiss, and blood roared through his head.

Lily's tongue eagerly tangled with his. Somehow she was on his lap, straddling him, her fine behind pressing against his throbbing erection. He couldn't stop the upward thrust of his hips. Lily moaned and wriggled closer, and he almost lost control.

"Easy," he said, lifting her up when he really wanted to rip off her jeans and panties and take her.

"Sorry." She settled back a little, then took his mouth with the same intensity that he'd captured hers.

He had to touch her. He slid his palms up her sides,

stopping at her breasts. Not sure if she wanted that, he hesitated.

Never taking her mouth from his, Lily guided his hands to her breasts. They were big and soft, a hint at paradise. But with her T-shirt and bra in the way, not nearly enough.

He let out a frustrated groan. "That shirt has got to go."

"Yours, too," she said.

In seconds he was bare-chested, and Lily was stripped to a cocoa-colored bra. Her nipples poked enticingly against the lace.

"Have mercy." His hands shaking, he unfastened the front clasp, pulled off the thing and tossed it aside. Her breasts were full, the nipples dusky pink and taut with arousal. A soft flush stained her chest. Desire. For him.

Overcome with feeling, Carter swallowed. "There are no words for your beauty."

"Thank you, Carter." She flashed a shy but proud smile.

He cupped her. Breathy, gasping, she arched back, thrusting her breasts fully into his hands.

Desperate to taste her, he licked and sucked each nipple. And quickly learned that she was ultrasensitive. He gentled his mouth and was rewarded with throaty sounds that drove him wild. There was no room on the sofa to lay her down or lie with her, so he pulled her onto the floor. His feet hit a pile of something. Ignoring everything but Lily, he kissed her again, then unbuttoned her jeans and tugged down the zipper. As the fly dropped open he slid his hand under the elastic of her panties. Moved past the soft curls and lower still.

Swallowing audibly, Lily opened her thighs. Carter fingered her slick heat, watching her face darken with need. She moaned and raised her hips off the floor, and it was all he could do to keep from ripping off her jeans and his slacks and sliding into her warmth. But this was about her.

He slipped two fingers inside her. "Does this feel good?"

"Oh, jeez, yes, but I'm about to climax."

"Do it, Lily. Let go." The instant he moved his thumb across her swollen nub, she convulsed around him.

Her face was flushed and her expression so openly passionate, the whole experience so erotic, he almost came with her. Only the thought of embarrassing himself kept him from losing control.

When she again lay still, Carter kissed her smooth belly. Lying beside her on the rug, he pulled her close. Her sweet woman smell was on his hand, marking him.

Wearing a contented smile, she touched his face. "That was…amazing."

Knowing she was thoroughly satisfied made the painful ache in his groin—what his friends back in high school referred to as blue balls—easier to bear. He kissed the tip of her nose. "I enjoyed it, too."

She glanced at his strained zipper. "Not as much as I did." Her hand slid downward. "Your turn."

Things had already gone way further than he'd intended. Hell, the two of them weren't even dating yet. Carter trapped her hand and pulled it to his lips. "Another time," he said, kissing her sensitive inner wrist.

"You're turning me on all over again."

Not what he needed to hear. He released her, then retrieved her bra and top. Handed them to her and picked up his own shirt.

By the time he'd shrugged into it, buttoned and tucked it in, Lily was dressed.

Except she wasn't wearing the bra. And if that wasn't

enough, her mouth was pink and slightly swollen from his kisses. Damned if he didn't want to pull her close and finish what they'd started. *Slow down, buddy.* He curled his hands into fists and kept them at his sides.

Man, he needed to leave. He was about to do just that when Lily gave him an anxious look.

"Are you sorry about what happened?" she asked, curling her toes into the carpet.

He realized he was frowning, and lightened his expression. "Not at all. I liked what we did. A lot." His traitorous eyes darted to her breasts. "I just didn't intend to get so carried away."

And they were right back to the question that had gotten him into trouble tonight.

"Did I convince you that I'm interested?"

CARTER HAD JUST GIVEN Lily a glimpse of heaven. She wanted him more than ever, so much that she was beyond caring about a possible broken heart. She was head over heels in love with him.

If only she knew what he felt for her. Desire, yes, but did he care as deeply as she did?

Fearing the answer, and wary of scaring him away, she kept her thoughts to herself and simply answered his question. "You're a very skilled and persuasive man."

"That's good to know." He looked pleased. Then glanced at his watch. "Whoa, it's late. I'm supposed to pick up Alex in five hours and I still need to get out my fishing gear. I'd better go. Walk me to the door?"

"Technically, this wasn't a date," she said as she opened the front door. "So anytime you want to come back again…"

His eyes glittered with heat. "I'll keep that in mind."

At his sensual look, her entire body warmed and stretched toward him. To keep from reaching for him, she grasped the doorjamb. The cool night air felt good on her hot face.

"And, Lily?"

"Yes, Carter?"

"From now on, if something bothers you, tell me."

"I will. Promise."

He touched her cheek. Hardly aware of her actions, she turned her face into his hand and kissed his palm.

"I'll call you," he said in a husky voice. "Good night. Sleep well."

"You, too."

In a daze she closed the door.

# Chapter Eight

"Morning," Alex said as he slid into the passenger seat.

Having only been up for twenty minutes, and not fully awake yet, Carter grunted.

As he rolled his CR-V down Alex's well-lit driveway, his friend glanced at him. "Man, you don't look so good. Out late partying?"

Oh, it'd been a party, all right. A very private party Carter would never forget. And he sure as hell wasn't sharing. "It's three-fricking-thirty in the morning." He scrubbed his hand over his chin, which was stubbly—he hadn't bothered to shave. "Who's awake at this hour? Can't even find a Starbucks open." He noted his friend's toothy grin. "What's got you so damned cheerful?"

"I'm a newlywed." Alex winked. "I'm happy most of the time."

Which probably had a good deal to do with the sex he was getting on a regular basis. Lucky bastard.

At the end of the driveway Carter frowned and checked the dark road for traffic. "You're disgusting."

"Jealous, huh." Alex chuckled. "I've been in your shoes, and I don't envy you. The single life gets old fast."

Carter fully agreed. He'd left Lily's a frustrated man, and after a few hours' fitful sleep and a cold shower, he still was.

Alex flipped on the map light and scanned the reservation for the fishing boat Carter had reserved, then glanced over at him. "Ginny wanted me to ask about your search for the right woman—wait." He squinted. "Is that a love bite on your neck?"

Damn, did it show? Carter tugged up the collar of his windbreaker. "None of your business."

"Ah," Alex said. "That explains the bad mood. She wouldn't put out, huh?"

Certain Lily would've made love with him, but not about to have this very personal conversation with his best bud, Carter merely said, "Have I ever been one to kiss and tell?"

"No need to say a word." Damned if Alex didn't flash his teeth again. "Your scowl says it all." When Carter swore softly, he quickly sobered. "You really like this woman. Gonna tell me her name? How'd you meet her?"

"You ask a lot of questions, and I haven't even had my coffee yet. She's a new client. I'm handling an audit for her. It's not till the middle of June, so we're not dating yet."

"But you're fooling around."

*And how.* Carter rolled his tense shoulders. "It shouldn't have happened."

And wouldn't again until after that audit. He felt like a jerk for crossing his own boundaries with Lily. But they'd both wanted it, and he wasn't sorry. Pleasuring Lily had been the most mind-blowing experience of his life. He hungered to do it again, and a whole lot more.

"A client? Man, that's not good."

"Think I don't know that?" Carter growled.

"Easy, buddy." Alex held up his hand, then snapped off the

light. A few moments of tense silence passed before he added, "It's not like you to get personally involved with a client."

How right he was. In the past Carter had been tempted a few times, but he'd always maintained a professional distance. That had changed with Lily. His grip on the wheel tightened and he called himself a few choice names.

"Quit beating yourself up, Carter. It's not illegal or anything."

Carter knew that, too. "Yeah, but it borders on unethical."

"She must be something else."

"Yeah." In no mood to talk about his feelings, he turned on the radio and cranked up the sound, putting an end to the conversation.

Neither of them said much again until Carter motored their rental boat to their favorite fishing area, about ten miles out, and Alex dropped anchor.

It was a quiet morning, on the chilly side. Too dark yet to see the mountains in the distance. Waves gently lapped the boat. Carter pulled in a fortifying breath of ocean air and took his favorite lure from his tackle box. In companionable silence, he and Alex tied their lures to their hooks.

It was a sure bet that for the next few hours he wouldn't think about Lily or anything but fishing. This was exactly what he needed. "I have a good feeling about this morning," he said. "We're gonna catch a mess of fish."

"I'm counting on it. So is Ginny. She bought extra freezer bags, and I cleaned the smoker."

Three hours later Alex had caught two big salmon. Carter, nothing. Not even a nibble. Frustrated, he shifted in his seat. "I'm about ready to throw in the towel."

"It's your mood, buddy. You're all tensed up. The fish can sense those things. You need to get laid."

"Tell me something I don't know." Carter glanced at the cloudless morning sky. "Ain't happening, not for a while."

"Look, if you're willing and she's willing… While we've been sitting here, waiting for the fish to bite, I've been thinking about your situation. If it were me…I'd go for it."

"You would?" Carter eyed his friend, who sold insurance to businesses and was about as straight-laced as a guy could be. "With a client."

Alex nodded. "It's not like you're gonna make a habit of it. This is a special case. You're already involved with the woman, right? Even if you two have sex, you'll still do the same outstanding job for her."

That was true.

"Maybe an even better job, once you clear your mind—if you get my meaning. At least talk it over with her."

"I'll think about it." The second the words were out of Carter's mouth, his pole jerked. "Yes!" Jumping to attention, he grabbed hold of the reel.

"What'd I tell you?" Alex grinned. "It's all about your mood."

"THESE ARE GREAT snickerdoodles," Carter said after polishing off several following dinner Sunday night. He and his mom were sitting at the dining-room table, drinking decaf and working their way through a plate of the cookies.

"You can thank Lily for that. She made them."

His mom would bring up Lily. Two days after their hot evening together, Carter couldn't stop thinking about her. Her passion, the way she'd come undone in his arms…

Not about to go there, he grabbed another cookie. "And just when did she do that?"

"Last week, when Hailey was napping and Lily didn't want to wake her. I was ready to mix up a batch of cookies and she wanted to learn, so I talked her through the recipe."

"Huh. She didn't mention that." But, hell, they'd had other things on their minds.

"Then you've talked to her?"

Not since Friday night, but he was planning to call soon. His mother was staring hard at him, making him uncomfortable, so he stood and began clearing the table. "She's a client, Mom."

"I'm your mother, and I know you too well to be fooled. She's more than that."

Carter narrowed his eyes. "Back off."

Uncowed by his glare and looking totally innocent, she shrugged. "All right, but let me say one more thing. You caught a forty-pound salmon, and both our freezers are full. Not that I'm not grateful, but there's only so much either of us can eat. Wouldn't it be nice to share some with Lily? With tourist season starting in just four days, she's working so hard. I know she'd welcome a night off and a good meal. Why don't you grill her a salmon steak? I'd be happy to watch Hailey."

After what had happened the other night, Carter wasn't about to do that. Being alone with Lily was way too tempting. He'd thought a lot about what Alex had said. But as much as he wanted her, it was best to wait. Even if it killed him.

"Good news," Lily said over a quick lunchtime sandwich Monday. She and Charity, both busy, hadn't spoken in days and were sitting on folding chairs in a sunny patch near her booth. "I hired a college sophomore, home for the summer, to work weekend nights." And with the season opening Thursday, not one second too soon. "Her name is Selena, and she's a sweetheart. Cindy's going to train her how to lock up, and I'll work with her, too."

"That's great."

Charity didn't sound like her normal, cheerful self. Lily studied her with a critical eye. She was wearing concealer that didn't quite cover the circles under her eyes. "You're dragging today," Lily said.

"I haven't been sleeping much."

With so much to do, who was? Of course, Lily had other reasons for her lack of sleep. Bursting to tell Charity what had happened between her and Carter, she leaned in close. "Wait'll you hear about—"

To her shock, Charity began to cry.

"What's wrong?" Lily asked.

"Trevor and I had a fight, and I'm so upset."

And here they'd been getting along so well. "I'm so sorry." Lily fished in her purse for a tissue and handed it over. "What happened?"

"Oh, Lily, I really screwed up! Trevor wanted to go out Saturday night, but I wanted to stay in. It's been so long since I've been with a man, and my feelings for Trevor were so intense...." She sniffed. "I wanted to take things to a new level."

Several friends from other booths walked by, casting curious glances at Charity and Lily. Charity blew her nose, then lowered her voice. "I wanted sex with my man. It was all I could think about. Even though it was early in the relationship, I thought I'd die if it didn't happen. You know?"

"I think I do," Lily said. It had been like that Friday night. She'd have done anything to make love with Carter.

The man certainly knew how to pleasure a woman. He'd stopped before they actually had sex, but what they'd shared… Her body went all hot and she squirmed in her chair. The entire weekend she'd felt this way, antsy and restless, wishing he'd stop by again. But Charity didn't need to hear about that now.

"So you and Trevor made love."

Charity gave an unhappy nod.

"Was the sex bad?"

"Actually, it was pretty darned spectacular. At least *I* thought so." Charity blew out a dejected breath. "Apparently Trevor didn't. Within fifteen minutes of finishing, we were fighting. He walked out and I haven't heard from him since."

"That's not good." Lily hadn't heard from Carter, either. But he'd gone fishing Saturday, and she'd been really busy. She knew he'd call soon—he'd said he would. "I wish I could think of the right thing to say. What did you fight about?"

"Something totally inane. He wanted to turn on the television and I wanted to talk and cuddle." Charity laughed without humor. "Pretty pathetic, huh."

"It *is* strange."

"Thing is, I know the fight had nothing to do with watching TV after sex. It's something else. I just wish I knew what was bothering him."

Thank goodness Carter wasn't like that. Lily counted her lucky stars that they were able to talk about anything and everything. She had no secrets from him and he had none from her. Being with a totally honest man was wonderfully refreshing.

"Maybe you should call him," Lily said. "And ask him point-blank what's wrong."

"I refuse to chase after Trevor." Up went Charity's chin.

"He picked the fight. *He* should call *me*." An instant later, her bravado faded into a look of sheer misery. "Shoot, I'm supposed to deliver a wind sock and chimes order at the yacht company on Wednesday. How will I ever face him?"

"You're both adults," Lily said. "Your business relationship is completely separate from what happened the other night." She wasn't sure she believed her own words, but Charity was listening closely. "I'm not saying chase him. I just think it's better to get everything out in the open."

"Maybe you're right. At least I'll think about it. No, he should make the first move." Charity compressed her lips. "I don't want to talk about this anymore. Tell me something fun. What's happening with Carter?"

"Well." Lily lowered her voice. "The other night we—"

Charity's eyes widened. "Don't tell me you two slept together?"

"No," Lily said. "But believe me, I'm thinking about it." Constantly.

"Ooh, and you haven't even started dating yet. That must have been some kiss the other day. Does Carter know?"

Charity was her best friend, so Lily decided to tell her everything. "Actually, he does. Friday night he stopped by and…we came close to making love. We stopped because we're not even dating yet, and won't be until after the audit."

"That's a long ways away. You don't have to be dating to have sex, you know."

"Carter thinks we should wait. But it's really hard."

"I hear you," Charity said. "If you want my advice, I say, what's a little sexual frustration? Take your time. I wish I had."

"I'M GLAD YOU CALLED." Holding her cell phone close, Lily snuggled into the sofa. She should be working, but she preferred to focus on Carter. This was the third evening in a row he'd phoned, and she'd started to look forward to their nightly conversations.

"Yeah, me, too."

His low, intimate voice thrummed through her and made her feel restless and needy. But after hearing what had happened with Charity, Lily knew Carter was right, that waiting was best. She'd told him, too, right after she'd filled him in on her best friend's fight with her boyfriend.

"All set for tomorrow?" he asked. The start of tourist season.

"As ready as I can be." For the first time in seven years, Lily dreaded the long hours. "I'm going to miss Hailey. I'm glad she has your mother to shower her with love and attention."

"Mom's pretty happy, too."

Lily smiled. Sharing things with Carter felt so right. Every day she fell more in love with him. Her feelings were the one thing she kept to herself. When the time was right, she'd tell him.

"Charity delivered an order to Trevor's office this afternoon," she said. "She was really nervous about it."

"How'd that go?"

"Not great. He claimed he was too busy to talk to her, and had his assistant handle the transaction. She's pretty broken up."

"That's a shame."

After spending an hour on the phone with her angry, sobbing friend, Lily fully agreed. "I just hope she'll be able to get some sleep tonight, because tomorrow's going to be crazy."

"What time do the booths officially open?"

"Nine." Which wasn't half-bad, since Hailey was up by seven-thirty. Lily would have time to feed and dress the baby and even play with her a little. "I'm meeting Selena, that college girl I hired, to show her the ropes. She'll be working with me for the first few mornings, then coming back to help Cindy close. I sure hope she works out."

"I know how hard it is to find good help. I went through two of the world's worst secretaries before I found Linda."

"You lucked out with her. She's the best." Lily considered her a friend now.

"She never lets me forget that, either."

His low chuckle was contagious, and Lily's own laughter bubbled out. She bumped the coffee table and her mother's late birthday card fell onto the carpet. Bending down, she retrieved it.

"You'll never guess who I heard from today."

"Janice?"

"I wish." Her sister was as impossible to reach as ever. "My mother finally sent me a birthday card. It's only two weeks late."

"You had a birthday recently? Why didn't I know about that?"

"The big three-oh. It was the thirtieth of April, before we met."

"No kidding. That's the same day—"

He broke off.

"Carter?"

"Someone I, uh, used to know was born on April thirtieth."

He sounded brusque. An old girlfriend, maybe? Lily wanted to know. She wanted to know *everything* about Carter.

Hoping he'd explain, she said, "Thanks for letting me complain about my mother. I feel like I can tell you anything."

"You can."

His tone was normal again, making her wonder if she'd imagined the tension. She waited for him to say the same thing, that he knew he could share everything with her, no problem.

He didn't.

Which bothered her, made her think he was hiding something. "You can tell me anything, too," she said.

"Thanks. I—" He broke off once more.

Leaving her curious. What had he been about to say? "Anything," she pressed. "No matter what."

"Look, if there's something you want to know, just ask."

Goodness, he was prickly. If he didn't want to talk about an old girlfriend, Lily wasn't about to pry. "No," she said. "I'm good for now."

"Great."

They chatted a few minutes more about this and that, but Lily couldn't dismiss the feeling that something was off, that Carter was keeping something important from her. Which was silly.

*It's all in my head,* she told herself. Yet she continued to stew, until the possibility that he was less than straightforward had her stomach churning. But as she lay in bed later, she decided she was jumping to conclusions. She and Carter had a relationship based on honesty. She trusted him completely. If there was something she should know, he'd tell her.

*Chapter Nine*

Early Monday evening Carter made his way toward Lily's booth, past hordes of adults and kids browsing and spending money on handcrafted items. It had been more than a week since he'd seen her, and tourist season was in full force. He was here to prep for the audit by observing her at work, he told himself, but looked forward to seeing her way too much.

Sure, they talked every night. Carter thoroughly enjoyed those conversations, but they weren't nearly enough. Especially now that she was so busy and so tired at night.

The one bad moment had happened the other evening, when she'd shared the date of her birthday. Which, incredibly, was the same as his daughter's, and a perfect segue to tell Lily about her. Thing was, the subject seemed too important to discuss over the phone, so he'd let the moment pass.

Now his secret ate at him. His daughter was a big part of him, even though he hadn't seen her since her birth. There was no way Lily would ever find out about her unless he told her. Still, not having his child in his life left a huge hole in his heart, and Lily deserved to know about that. Every day his conscience bothered him more.

*Tell her now,* urged a voice in his head. Carter set his jaw. This wasn't the time or place. He'd tell her soon, he promised himself.

He caught sight of Lily in her booth and for a few seconds stood back, out of her view, watching as she chatted up a pair of middle-aged women and their husbands. Lily said something that made everyone laugh, and Carter knew the tourists were like every other person she met—dazzled by her charm.

As Lily smiled and pointed out various pieces of jewelry, the slanting sun bathed her in soft light. Her eyes sparkled with life, and that smile…

Overcome with an emotion he didn't understand, Carter swallowed thickly. Barely containing his need to be with her, he waited impatiently until the shoppers walked away. Then he strode forward, into Lily's line of vision.

When she saw him, her face lit up. His heart seemed to swell in his chest.

"Carter. What a wonderful surprise."

"How's it going?" he said.

"Mostly nonstop. It makes the time fly. What brings you here?"

"Observing the businesswoman at work, for the audit."

"Observe away. If what's happened so far is any indication of the rest of the season, look out." Her dimples flashed. "I track my sales, and so far I'm ahead of last year."

"That's great." She made terrific jewelry, but Carter figured the real reason for her success was that no one could resist her. "Why don't you and Hailey come over tomorrow night for dinner?" he said, surprising himself.

Her eyes widened. "You want us at your *house?*"

Now that he'd asked, he realized he did. He wanted to show Lily what success had earned him, to watch her face when she saw his home. It was a good place to explain about his daughter, too. His gut tensed at the thought. He'd decide later.

He nodded. "This time of year, you probably never have time to cook, and I grill a mean salmon steak. Part of my catch from when Alex and I went fishing."

His mother would be so pleased. But Carter didn't intend to tell her about this.

"I'd like to," Lily said. "But I can't leave the booth until Cindy and Selena show up at seven. Then I have to pick up Hailey at your mom's. We get so little time together these days, and I try to play with her before she goes down for the night." She rubbed at a scratch on the counter before looking at him. "And there's the other thing."

He knew exactly what she was thinking. That it was dangerous for them to be alone. Carter agreed, but looking into Lily's big, expressive eyes, he no longer cared. He wanted her too much to wait. Sooner or later it was going to happen, so why not sooner?

"We both have to eat, and you wouldn't believe all the fish in my freezer," he said. "You and Hailey will be doing me a favor by helping me get rid of some of it."

"She probably won't eat anything that late. She doesn't stay awake past eight-thirty. That won't give you and me much time."

"It will if you put her down in one of the spare bedrooms."

*Bedroom.* The very word charged Carter's imagination. The thought of him and Lily in his king-size bed… It was enough to make his palms sweat.

By the blush on Lily's face, she was thinking along similar lines.

"If I come over, you know what will happen," she said. "Shouldn't we wait?"

"I'm tired of waiting." Carter took her hands in his. "I want to make love with you at my house, in my bed," he said for her ears only.

Her eyes darkened. "Are you sure?"

"It's all I think about."

"But you said… What about the audit?"

Carter gazed into her eyes. "I'm good at my job. Us being together won't change that."

"Then, yes, I'll be there."

"Great." He let out a relieved breath. "Bring Hailey's pajamas, because you two are spending the night."

"In that case I'll bring her crib, too."

The naked hunger on Lily's face promised a night of passion, and it was all Carter could do to keep from pulling her out of the booth and finding someplace private right now.

A woman, two couples and several teenage girls were headed toward the booth. "Customers," Lily said, pulling her hands free. "I'll see you tomorrow night."

"I'll be waiting," Carter said. "One more thing—don't mention this to my mother."

Whistling, he walked away.

ON TUESDAY AFTERNOON, having cut her last class of the day, Randi Gerrity stood at the Fort Dodge, Iowa, Greyhound ticket window. "How do I get to Halo Island, Washington?" she said, trying to look and sound as if she was tons older. As if she was eighteen. Which she wouldn't be for almost a year.

"Halo Island. That's in the San Juans in the Pacific

Northwest, right?" The overweight clerk turned away to tap on his computer. "There's no Greyhound service to the island. You'll take a bus to Bellingham, Washington. From there you'll transfer to a shuttle or a train to Anacortes, Washington. Then you'll catch the ferry to Halo Island. It'll take a good two days."

"Oh." Randi didn't hide her disappointment. That sounded complicated. "How much will it all cost?"

"One way or round trip?"

Uncertain of the answer, she hesitated. That depended on her father, a man who'd never shown the slightest interest in her. A man who, until recently, she'd thought was dead. "One way, I guess."

The man behind the counter added up the amount and told her. It wasn't cheap. Randi almost had enough for the bus ticket, but not the train or ferry. A few more weekly paychecks from the grocery store where she worked and she would, though.

"You're awfully young to be traveling by yourself." The clerk squinted at her through his dirty glasses. "You a runaway?"

"No!" Randi stiffened, mostly because she was scared. In a sense, she *was* running away. From a mother who was so wrapped up in her new husband she no longer wanted Randi around. Neither did Richard, her new stepfather. He didn't like kids, especially her. "I'm eighteen," she lied. "And my father lives on Halo Island."

In a recent fight, her mother had blurted out that Randi's father was alive and that maybe Randi should go live with him. After thinking him dead her whole life, Randi still couldn't get over this amazing news. She hadn't believed her mom until she'd checked the Net. Carter Boyle wasn't exactly a common name, and she'd found his Web page easily enough. Now she knew where she'd gotten her height and her pale blue eyes.

"He's an accountant," she said. She wasn't sure what accountants did, but it had something to do with taxes. Which sounded complicated and also boring, and meant he was really smart.

She was all mixed up, hating him since he obviously didn't care about her at all, but still wanting to meet him. She hated her mom, too, for not telling the truth a long time ago.

"Does he know you're coming?" Mr. Nosy asked.

"Um, yeah." Another lie. As far as Randi knew, her mom hadn't been in contact with her father in ages. And *he* sure hadn't been in touch. "I have to go to work now, but I'll be back in a few weeks with the money."

She'd ask for more hours and work as much as possible. Because she *had* to leave here, and the sooner the better.

But what if her father didn't want her, either?

Randi wouldn't let herself worry about that. Because now that her mom was married to Richard, and her grandparents were dead, she had no one else to turn to.

WHEN LILY STOPPED to pick up Hailey at Henri's the following evening, the older woman greeted her with her usual warmth. "Tired?"

It had been a long day, and after being on her feet for a good ten hours dealing with nonstop customers, Lily should've been exhausted. But she was too keyed up about the night ahead. Not wanting Henri to suspect a thing—she'd promised Carter, and besides, this was none of his mother's business—she offered a smile. "I'm okay."

"I made too much meat loaf tonight. You've been work-ing such long hours. Hailey's happy playing on the floor and could easily entertain herself for a while longer. Would you like to stay and have dinner?"

An offer Lily would've jumped at, if not for her plans with Carter. Dinner followed by making love… Only with effort did she stifle her growing anticipation. "Could I take a rain check?" she asked.

"You *are* tired. I understand. You and Hailey are as dear to me as family, so anytime you want a home-cooked meal, just ask."

The words melted Lily's heart. Henri was such a caring, honest and straightforward person. The opposite of Lily's own mom, and exactly the kind of mother Lily had always longed for. "Thank you."

"For what?"

"For being wonderful." Filled with emotion, she hugged her.

Henri squeezed back. When they pulled apart, she flushed with pleasure. "If I'd known a dinner offer would earn me a hug, I'd have invited you sooner. I could give you some meat loaf to take home."

"It's not just the offer," Lily said. Her heart was so full and she was so excited about the night ahead, she simply couldn't contain herself. "It's just… My mother never has been honest with me. I treasure the way you say what you mean and speak your mind."

Henri nodded. "You can depend on that."

"And I do. You're a good friend and I can tell you taught Carter well. A truly honest man is hard to find."

"Thank you." Henri's eyes narrowed shrewdly. "Are you trying to tell me something about you and Carter?"

"You mean, do I like him as more than my accountant?" Lily nodded. "I do. Carter doesn't know it yet, but I think I'm falling in love with him."

"Oh, honey, that makes me so happy. My son doesn't talk to me about his romantic interests, so he hasn't said, but I think he cares for you, too."

Little did Henri know… And if Carter realized Lily and his mother were having this conversation, he'd probably pass out. "Don't say anything to him, okay?"

Henri winked. "You have my word."

CARRYING HAILEY ON HER hip, and light-headed now that she was finally here, Lily climbed the stained wood steps to Carter's front door. His modern glass-and-wood house stood high on a bluff, and though there were other homes nearby, the tall fir trees around the perimeter of the yard gave the place a feeling of seclusion and privacy.

"Here we go," she told Hailey as she knocked on the door.

While they waited, she thought briefly of Charity. Except for the uncomfortable business call at the yacht club the other day, her friend had yet to hear from Trevor. What if Carter pulled away emotionally after tonight? The thought scared Lily a little.

Then again… "Carter and I aren't like Charity and Trevor," she told Hailey. "We don't have secrets and we talk things through."

Except for that one time on the phone the other night, when she'd sensed he was hiding something. But that had all been in her head, and why dredge up groundless worries now? *Nerves,* she assured herself—but that didn't help at all.

Carter opened the door wearing a polo shirt that hugged

his broad shoulders, and a chef's apron over faded jeans. "Hi," he said, his gaze warm and intimate.

With that look her misgivings vanished. The pale blue of his shirt was the same color as his eyes. And that sexy smile? The man was utterly irresistible. If not for Hailey, Lily would've gladly skipped dinner and fallen into his arms.

Hailey, who was just as gaga over him, made a loud, happy noise and reached out her chubby arms.

"Hey there, pip-squeak." Carter took the baby, then ruffled her hair.

"What a beautiful setting and a gorgeous house," Lily said, stepping into the entry. "Plus, something smells really good."

"That's a frozen potato casserole. The only home-cooked part of tonight is the salmon. Where's the crib?"

"In the trunk of my car. I couldn't carry it and Hailey. It wasn't easy keeping this a secret from your mom."

"But necessary. I'll grab the crib, and show you around when I get back." He handed over Hailey. "If you two want to wait for me in the kitchen…" He gestured down a hall. "Or relax in the living room."

"I'll be in the kitchen." Too restless to sit, Lily wandered around the kitchen, which was almost as big as her entire house. And ultramodern. A big maple table and six chairs sat in front of a large window. But that wasn't all.

"Look at the pretty bleached wood cabinets and the fancy stainless steel appliances, Hailey. And this huge fridge? We could fit ours inside it with room to spare, huh?"

"Booloo," Hailey said.

"I'm impressed, too. It's all tidied up, just like his office."

The man was a total neatnik, a trait Lily envied. She tried to keep her place organized, but the clutter seemed to reproduce on its own. No doubt after seeing her houseboat,

Carter figured she was a totally disorganized person. The thought dampened her spirits.

On the other hand, as clean and beautiful as his kitchen was, Lily saw no personal touches here. No magnets on the fridge, no apron hanging on the back door hook, not even a notepad by the phone. This could've been a Realtor's model home.

Carter probably spent most of his time at work. No doubt the house would start to look lived in after he married and started his family. Lily imagined herself as the mother of his children. As his wife. *I shouldn't,* she counseled herself. But she was in love with the man, and everything that was happening between them pointed to a long-term relationship. She simply couldn't help herself.

Humming and keeping Hailey on her hip, she stood at the window, which faced an expansive, fenced backyard. She noted the smoking grill on the wraparound deck. Way beyond, the sea and the mountains.

"His view is as good as ours," she said to Hailey. "Since he's a good ten feet above the water, maybe better."

"I'm glad you like it."

"Carter!" Lily spun toward him. "I didn't hear you come back inside."

He set the crib by the door. He was smiling, but not quite as warmly as before. If she didn't know him so well she'd have missed the fine tension in his shoulders. Was he having doubts?

She had to know. "Carter? Have you changed your mind?"

"No," he said, his gaze flitting over her. "But we need to talk."

The ominous words filled the air and settled heavily in her chest. "What about?" she asked, careful to remain cheerful.

He nodded at Hailey. "Later."

"Okay," Lily said, thoroughly confused.

"The coals won't be ready for a while. This is a good time to show you and Hailey her room and the rest of the house. Why don't we start upstairs."

"Ga." Hailey reached for him.

"Sure, I'll take you, pip-squeak." Settling the baby in the crook of one arm, he grasped the crib with the other. "Follow me."

"You've got Hailey," Lily said. "I'll take the crib."

"You worked all day. It's no problem for me to carry both."

As Carter led her through the kitchen, her mind whirled. Maybe he wanted a short fling, nothing more. He'd run into an old girlfriend and decided he wanted to get serious with her—or he'd met someone new. He and Lily were too different to have a relationship. There were dozens of possibilities, all pointing to an unhappy ending.

Lily didn't want a broken heart! She did have some pride. Carter would never know her true feelings for him.

In the formal dining room the chandelier glowed softly above the table set for two, providing an intimate feel that seemed at odds with the heart-to-heart she imagined was to come.

Okay, maybe she was overreacting. *Talking is good,* she reminded herself. Certainly better than holding things in. Yet she couldn't help thinking that the passionate night she'd dreamed of might not happen.

"This place is huge," she said, following Carter up a wide, carpeted staircase.

His shoulder and back muscles bunched as he cradled Hailey and hefted the portable crib. Such a big, beautiful, capable man.

"Yep, there's plenty of space," he said at the top of the stairs. "There are four bedrooms up here."

"Wow." Lily bit her lip to keep from asking him why he needed so much room.

"Perfect for a family, don't you think?" he said, as if reading her thoughts.

Was it possible he wanted to make a family with her? Lily's heart seemed to stutter in her chest, but Carter's expression was unreadable. Which was not a good sign. Yesterday she'd been certain he wanted a relationship. Now doubts filled her.

He headed for the bedroom at the far end of the hall. "I thought we'd put Hailey down in here."

The large room had a wall-size picture window that faced the water. Despite a queen-size bed and two reading chairs, there was ample room for a crib.

"Snafoo," Hailey said.

"That means wow," Lily interpreted. "She's never slept in a room this big."

"She's got her own bathroom, too."

Hailey reached out, and Lily gladly took her. The baby's little arms wrapped around Lily's neck, warming the cold places caused by her uncertainty.

Carter seemed oblivious of the havoc he'd set off inside her. He set up the crib, then showed Lily the two additional guest bedrooms, equally large and sharing a bathroom.

"My bedroom is at the other end of the hall," he said, walking her there.

Her confusion made her feel awkward, and she held tight to Hailey. But one glimpse of Carter's master suite and she forgot her uneasiness.

"Your own private deck, and a sitting room with a fireplace. And look at all the books on these bookshelves. This is spectacular!"

His chest seemed to swell with pride, and he flashed a pleased grin.

She peeked into the bathroom. It was hard to miss the huge shower and the soaker tub for two. Plenty of room for lovers to bathe and do other interesting and highly erotic things to each other.

Lily's cheeks burned. She could feel Carter's gaze. Afraid of what she might see in his eyes, she wiped drool from Hailey's chin. "The coals are probably ready," she said. "Maybe we should go back downstairs."

"Anything wrong?" he asked, peering at her.

*I'm nervous about what you're going to tell me.* Not about to admit that, she forced a smile and shook her head. "It's been a while since lunch," she said.

Not that she could eat a thing right now. Her stomach was in knots.

"In that case, I'd best put the fish on the grill. I'll give you a superfast tour of the main floor."

He quickly showed her around, ending in the spacious living room with its big windows, cozily lit by elegant floor lamps.

"Care for wine before dinner?" Carter said. "This time we'll actually drink it."

His eyes met hers and she knew he was thinking of the last time they'd been alone together, in her houseboat. That night they'd never even tasted the wine.

Tonight Lily needed the alcohol to steady her nerves. "A glass would be nice," she said.

And she was ready to sit down. While Carter headed off to pour the wine, she settled Hailey on the small patterned rug that lay over the thick carpet. "Enjoy yourself, sweetie, because soon it'll be your bedtime."

Though maybe Lily ought to keep her up a little later tonight. Anything to put off the dreaded talk. In need of a distraction, she tugged down her skirt and knelt on the rug. She pulled the caterpillar rattle Hailey loved and a handful of other toys from the diaper bag. Tonight the baby wanted to be tickled. As Lily indulged her, her delighted laughter filled the room. Soon Lily was laughing, too.

How she loved this child!

Carter returned with two glasses of wine.

"There's nothing as magical as a baby's laugh," he said, plunking himself down on the ottoman.

It was such a sweet thing to say. And as foolish as it was, Lily loved him more than ever for saying it.

He handed her a glass, then raised his own. "To tonight," he said, his eyes far too somber.

Scared all over again, she tilted her glass toward him. "Tonight." *May my heart stay whole.*

Suddenly Hailey moved into a crawl position.

Thrilled, Lily set down her glass. "Look, Carter! She's about to crawl."

Carter chuckled. "You're something else, pip-squeak."

Squealing with glee, the baby beamed at them both.

For one wishful moment Lily fantasized that Hailey was hers and Carter's, that they were a family and this was their home.

But Janice was Hailey's mother. And who knew what would happen with Carter? The baby collapsed onto her tummy.

"I'd best grill the fish," Carter said.

"Can I do anything to help?"

"Relax and play with Hailey."

Lily decided to do just that. All too soon she'd find out what was on Carter's mind.

## Chapter Ten

The grill sputtered and hissed and smoked, making Carter's eyes water. Moving out of range, he stared at the water.

The sun was sinking toward the horizon. In the distance someone's dog barked and a child's voice called out. A typical spring evening, perfect for romance with a warm, willing woman. With Lily.

She liked the house and seemed impressed. That felt good. Even better was the way she and Hailey softened the house and made it feel cozier. Like a home.

Lily was easy to read. The hunger in her expression as she glanced around his bedroom had stirred the fires simmering inside him. He wanted her so badly, he ached. Especially a certain part of him. He was semi-hard. Had been all day. Really, since she'd first walked into his office.

He was more than ready to make love with her. Before it happened, though, he meant to tell her about his daughter. Weeks had passed since he and Lily had first met, with more than a few missed opportunities to share what he would tonight. He wondered what she'd say and what she'd think of him once she knew.

What if she stopped looking at him as if he was special?

Changed her mind about making love with him? His very soul shuddered, and he considered letting the matter go.

But that was the cowardly route, and Carter was no coward. He'd be as honest with Lily as she was with him, and take his lumps. The second Hailey went to bed he'd share his sorry past.

The decision eased his conscience, and for the first time in days, he felt as if he could breathe deeply. Yet at the same time the muscles in his neck and shoulders tensed uncomfortably.

He'd never dreaded anything so much.

AN HOUR LATER Carter stood at the kitchen sink, washing up. Dinner had gone well, with Lily feeding Hailey bites of salmon, even though the little girl had eaten at his mother's. She made her usual joyous noises, which made Lily smile. Carter had managed a grin or two, but inside he was a jangle of nerves.

Now Lily was upstairs, putting the baby to bed. When she walked down the stairs, he'd finally tell her everything. At the thought, his mouth went dry.

He was in the living room, nursing a gin on the rocks to steady his nerves—it wasn't working—when Lily came down the steps.

"She's asleep," she said.

"That's good. Want a drink?" He nodded at the bottle.

"No, thanks." She hesitated in the doorway. "You said you wanted to talk?"

Trust her to get straight to the point. One look at her pinched, frightened face and Carter forgot his own fears.

He hadn't meant to scare her. *He* was the one with something to lose, yet somehow he'd sent the wrong message.

Wanting to reassure her, he patted the sofa cushion beside him. "Come and sit down."

Lily shook her head and stayed where she was, her hands ceaselessly twisting her bracelets. "If you'd rather we leave, please just say so. I'm a big girl. I understand that sometimes people change their minds—"

She broke off and chewed her lip.

Carter hadn't expected this. Not sure what she meant, he frowned. "What are you trying to say?"

"You seem so tense and serious, and now that Hailey's asleep, you want to talk. I thought… Maybe you don't want me here, after all."

Where in hell had that come from? "Nothing could be further from the truth." He stood, went to her and clasped her hands. "There is no one else, Lily," he said, touching his forehead to hers. "You're the woman for me, and I hope we're together for a long, long time."

"Really?" The worry faded from her eyes, and sheer joy lit her face. "*That's* what you wanted to say?" Laughing, she pulled back to touch his cheek. "Talk about looking for trouble. You have no idea how relieved I am."

She twined her hands around his neck, and it was all he could do to keep from starting what his body urged him to do.

*No.* First things first. He needed to explain about his daughter. He untangled her arms from his neck and guided her to the sofa. "There's more," he said, gently pushing her down and joining her.

"Tell me later. Right now, I *have* to show you how happy you've made me, and how much I want what you want." She scooted onto his lap.

Fire pulsed through his groin and his brain began to cloud.

*Tell her now, before things get too hot!* his conscience screamed.

But she slid her palms up his chest and stretched up to kiss him. Her sweet behind teased his crotch, and bam! He was rock-hard.

Blood roared through his veins. The instant her lips touched his, every thought in his head vanished except the one urging him to finally make Lily his.

CARTER'S MOUTH WAS HARD and demanding, and Lily eagerly met every kiss. Their tongues tangled and mated, the way she and Carter soon would. Need flooded her and she was damp between the legs. Aching to get closer, she straddled him.

Carter groaned and grasped her hips with hot hands. Raising her up, he ground his erection against her.

And suddenly, she was on the verge of climaxing. "Make love to me now," she whispered.

"Our first time should be in a bed," he said. "Let's go upstairs."

He moved her off his lap, stood and tugged her hand.

But Lily's limbs felt so weak and heavy, she couldn't move. "I'm not sure I can walk," she said.

"Then I'll take you."

Sweeping her into his arms, he carried her up the stairs, stopping along the way for passionate kisses. At some point he set her down to strip away her dress. She stepped out of her sandals and helped Carter out of his shirt.

Heat and desire seemed to pulse between them, and Lily had no idea how they made it to his room.

Light from the silver moon shone through the window and guided them to the bed. Carter ripped off the spread.

He kicked out of his shoes, removed his socks, then faced her, his eyes glittering with passion.

"Let's get naked," he said.

Bathed in moonlight, her gaze fastened on the man she loved, Lily unhooked her bra.

Carter unbuckled his belt and his fly. As she tossed the bra aside, he shed his jeans. His erection strained against his boxers.

Weak with need, Lily shimmied out of her panties. The bracelets went next, clinking softly as they hit the rug. Carter's boxers dropped to the floor and he sidestepped them.

At last they were both naked.

Carter was gloriously aroused. And all hers.

"You're beautiful," he said in a hoarse voice. "I want to hold you."

Dazed and filled with warmth and tenderness, Lily walked into his arms.

His erection pressed against her stomach. She laid her head on his solid chest and heard the thud-thud of his heart. His strong arms cradled her. Love and desire for this man filled her completely. She melted against him.

"You feel so good." Carter bowed his head and kissed her shoulder at the sensitive place where it joined her neck.

A fierce hunger drowned out her tender feelings. Reaching between them, she boldly cupped his thick, jutting length.

Carter groaned and moved backward to the bed.

Suddenly Lily was on her back, staring up at him, her hands pinned over her head.

"This is more like it." A wicked smile curled his lips before he leaned down. His mouth and clever tongue sent shivers of pleasure through first one nipple, then the other, until she was crazed with wanting and impatient for more.

"Touch me," she pleaded, opening her legs. "There."

"Oh, I plan to, when I'm through here." He gently grazed each nipple with his teeth.

Moaning, she leaned up and nipped his earlobe. He raised his head to look at her. His eyes smoldered.

"You're so passionate," he whispered. "I love that about you. Love your breasts, too."

He blew his breath over her wet, sensitive peaks and she trembled.

Molten fire settled in her belly, and she could barely speak. "I like the way you show your appreciation." *And I love you,* she added silently, sensing that she shouldn't blurt out her feelings just now.

At last he knelt between her legs. Holding her ankles in his hands, he kissed the inside of one knee, then slowly kissed a trail up her inner thigh, moving closer to the place that most craved his attention.

Urging him nearer, Lily arched her hips. The stubborn man refused to be hurried. When she was ready to die of frustration, he parted her inner lips and slipped two fingers inside her. Waiting for his mouth, she tensed. Finally, *finally,* his tongue swirled across her aching nub. She wanted to weep with relief. As he nipped and tongued her, she almost went over the edge.

"No," she gasped, pushing his head away. "This time, I won't climax without you."

She tumbled him onto his back. Took his velvety head into her mouth and suckled him gently while she stroked his stiff length.

"Sweet mercy," he moaned, cupping the back of her head.

An instant later he abruptly lifted her away. "Much as I like that, if you don't stop it won't be pretty."

Lily understood. Her body literally ached to join with his. "Then please," she said, "put us both out of our misery."

"Hang on one sec." Jerking open the drawer in the bedside table, he pulled out a condom. Tore open the packet and sheathed himself.

Covering her with his body, he kissed her savagely and in one smooth stroke entered her. She felt her body stretch to accommodate him.

Giving her a moment to adjust, Carter held still, his own body all coiled tension.

As he began to move, Lily moaned. "You're so big."

He stilled. "Am I hurting you?"

"No, you're… This is perfect." And she loved him so. Right now, nothing mattered but her and Carter and the intense pleasure they shared. She pressed the small of his back with her palms. "Please, don't hold back."

"Like this?" He pushed in hard. Deep.

"Yes." Gasping, she met him eagerly. "Again," she begged, gripping his hips with her thighs.

"My. Pleasure."

Each thrust added to the delicious tension pulsing inside her. Then, *yes!* She climaxed with a pleasure so intense, the world faded.

"Lily," Carter called out, joining her with a last, satisfying drive.

When the room righted itself again, her head was pillowed on Carter's chest. His arm was around her, cupping her tightly against his side.

"That was amazing," he said.

"The best sex I've ever had."

He kissed her forehead. "That makes me feel great."

"I love you," she said, unable to contain herself.

The instant the words were out, Carter tensed.

Lily closed her eyes and wished she'd kept her mouth shut.

*I LOVE YOU.* No lover had ever said those words to Carter, not since Darla back in high school. But the mother of his daughter had only mouthed the words. Lily wouldn't say them unless she really did love him.

"I shouldn't have said that, huh?"

It was still light enough to see her worried frown. He kissed her tenderly. "I'm glad you did."

Her love felt so damn fantastic. There was no way he'd ruin the sweetness of the moment by telling her about his past. Not now. Even if his conscience was stabbing him like a son of a bitch.

Carter hadn't planned on making love until after he told her. But that had changed when she'd kissed him. He'd eagerly put off sharing his secret for the most intense pleasure of his life.

Now it was too late. Turned out he was a coward. And a hell of a mess he'd made. Cursing himself for taking the easy road, he propped his arms under his head and stared at the dark ceiling.

"Carter?" Lily levered herself up on her elbow and eyed him, two vertical lines creasing the space between her eyebrows. "What's wrong?"

"Nothing."

"I know you, and I can feel that something's bothering you. Does this have anything to do with what you wanted to say earlier?"

Not about to answer that question tonight, he forced a light tone. "Forget about that for now. I'll be right back."

He pulled the sheet and blanket over her, then padded into the bathroom. After closing the door behind him, he flipped on the light, but didn't glance into the mirror. There was no way he could face himself.

*Tomorrow,* he promised, and this time he meant it. He'd stop by Lily's booth when she got off at seven, take her someplace quiet and private, and talk to her before she picked up Hailey. He'd call his mother, explain what he wanted to do, and ask her to keep the baby late to give him the time he needed. That'd work.

He'd tricked his conscience so many times, it didn't believe him, and he wasn't in the best mood when he returned to bed with a warm washcloth.

"For you," he said, handing it to her.

"Thanks." She flashed a brief smile. "Are you sure nothing's wrong?"

Realizing he was frowning, he forced a grin. "Nothing, except I want to see you again tomorrow night."

"I'd like that, too," she said.

Her expression softened and turned tender, and Carter relaxed. Somewhat. His secret lay heavy in his gut, but he just couldn't tell her now.

There was only one way to drown out the guilt. Make love with Lily again. Depending on her reaction to his sorry story, tonight might be their only night together.

Pushing away the miserable thought, he turned to her. "I have a problem, Lily."

He stroked her sensitive nipple. She sucked in a breath, and his own body hardened with need.

"Y-yes?" she said, arching under his touch.

This was better. Carter smiled to himself. "I can't decide

if I should make love with you next in bed, in the tub or the shower."

"That's easy," she said. "Let's try all three."

## Chapter Eleven

At lunchtime the following day, Lily's body was still aglow from her passionate night with Carter. A night she would never forget. Not only was he a generous, considerate lover, he also wanted to see her again tonight. Although he hadn't exactly said he loved her, she knew he cared.

She ought to be the happiest woman alive. And she was…except for a vague uneasiness, a tiny pang that no amount of self-assurance could banish.

She couldn't put her finger on exactly what bothered her. Had she imagined the odd something she heard every now and then in Carter's voice, or his barely masked tension, or the way he'd kept her too preoccupied with sex for any serious conversation?

Not that she minded. Making love with Carter was fantastic, and the pleasure intensified each time. Maybe she was imagining things. She hoped so—and wished she knew.

It was a slow morning, with way too much time for brooding. In need of a break and a friendly ear, Lily retrieved the sandwich she'd picked up after dropping off Hailey this morning. Dear, sweet Hailey. Thank goodness the baby couldn't talk, because she'd no doubt have told

Henri where her auntie had slept last night. Lily wasn't up to the older woman's knowing looks or comments.

Sandwich and purse in hand, she headed for the booth next to hers, where Kelly, a friendly, fortyish woman, sold beach art. "Will you keep an eye on my place while I eat a quick lunch?"

Kelly, who was artfully attaching shells to a small watercolor, shrugged. "No problem."

"Thanks. I'll be back in thirty minutes, tops. I've got my cell, so if it gets busy, call me." Lily made her way to Charity's booth, waving at friends along the way. "Can you get away for lunch?" she asked. "Since it's so warm and beautiful today, I thought we could sit on the beach."

"After my slow morning, that sounds perfect," Charity said. "Let me ask Jack, next door, to watch my booth."

Minutes later, amid dozens of other beachgoers, Lily and Charity were seated on the sand, facing the ocean, watching the easy waves and munching their sandwiches.

At least, Charity was. Lily couldn't work up much of an appetite.

Squinting in the bright sun, her friend eyed her. "You're awfully quiet. Something's bothering you."

Lily nodded. "I spent the night at Carter's."

"Uh-oh, that doesn't sound good. Weren't you two going to wait?"

"We changed our minds."

"Apparently, you shouldn't have. What'd he do, pull a Trevor?"

"Pick a fight and walk out? Nothing like that."

"That's a definite plus. Bad chemistry?"

"Actually, we're great together." And then some. "It's just…I'm not sure, but something doesn't feel quite right."

"I'm not following you."

"It's hard to explain. All I know is, Carter said he wanted to talk. But we sort of got distracted—my fault—and we never did."

As incredible as that first time had been, Lily wished she'd curbed her impatience long enough to listen.

"And you think whatever he wanted to say is behind this odd feeling of yours."

"Exactly," Lily said. "Later I tried to bring up the subject, but we were, um, occupied all night, and we never got around to talking."

"All night, huh?" Charity looked wistful. "I'm so jealous. Seems like ages since I've spent the whole night with a man. Darn that Trevor for being a jerk. If he'd just call, you know?"

"Focus, Charity. I need some help here."

"Sorry. You don't think Carter is seeing someone else at the same time? Or that he's one of those guys who can't commit?"

If so, Lily was certain he'd have said as much from the start. "Neither one. What do you think I should do?"

"Maybe you're overreacting. He probably wanted to tell you that you're the first woman to spend the night at his place, or something sweet like that."

"That's what I keep telling myself. I trust Carter completely." Which was true, but didn't ease Lily's anxieties.

"And yet you're filled with doubts. Are you seeing him again tonight?"

Lily nodded.

"All right then, here's what you'll do. Practice what you're always preaching—get down and get honest. *Ask* him if something is wrong, and what he wanted to say last night. Whatever it is, if you two really trust each other, you'll work it out."

Lily had done just that last night, but they'd been too busy to talk. Tonight would be different. "I will," she said. "Thanks for the advice."

"That's what friends are for. I want you to be happy. One of us should, right? Once your problems are settled, ask Carter if he knows any decent single guys. Because I'm through waiting around for Trevor to come to his senses." Charity glanced at her watch, then popped the last of her turkey wrap into her mouth. "We've been gone almost twenty minutes. We should get back in case business picks up soon. Today has been dead. And after the season started out so strong…"

"I'm not worried. This is just one of those days." Lily tossed the remains of her sandwich into the trash.

She wasn't back in the booth five minutes before her cell phone rang. She glanced at the LED, surprised to see Janice's name. And also leery. Her sister's track record for good-news phone calls wasn't the best.

"Hey, Janice," she said, leaning on the counter.

"Oh. Hi, Lily. Aren't you working? I was, um, hoping to get your voice mail."

Not a great way to start a conversation. Lily couldn't stifle her sigh of irritation. "I'm at work now. What is it this time? No, let me guess. You're not going to pick up Hailey at the end of the month."

"Jeez, you're grouchy. Maybe I should call back later and leave a message—"

"Don't you dare hang up. For once in your life, be an adult and just say what you have to say."

Lily had never spoken so bluntly, and she could hear her sister's gasp of surprise.

"Okay, but you're not going to like this. I've been doing a lot of thinking, and…"

Janice broke off and Lily knew that whatever she was about to say, it wouldn't be good. Filled with dread, she waited—a full five seconds.

"I've decided to give up Hailey," Janice said.

Never had Lily imagined this. She was momentarily speechless. Then she frowned. "There must be something wrong with the phone because I thought you said you're giving up Hailey. You wouldn't do that."

"I can and I am," Janice replied softly. "I'm not cut out to be a mother, and we both know it. Hailey's better off without me. I…I want you to adopt and raise her."

"Are you out of your mind?" Lily shouted. Noting Kelly's curious expression across the way, she lowered her voice. "You're doing drugs, aren't you?"

"You know I stay away from that stuff. I'm as straight and sane as you are."

Suddenly drained and sad, Lily sagged against the counter. "But, Janice, Hailey is your daughter, your flesh and blood. She's the most precious, sweet little girl ever, and she has so much love to give. You can't do this. You can't. Otherwise, you're no better than our father."

"Do *not* try to guilt me out of this, Lily. Our ass of a father has nothing to do with my decision. This is something I've thought about since Hailey was born. It's only now that I'm strong enough to do it. My mind's made up, and I'm not changing it. If you don't want Hailey, I'll contact social services and let them find her a home."

How could Janice be so heartless and cold? "Don't do

that! When you come back we'll sit down and talk, maybe find you a counselor to—"

"I'm not coming back," Janice said, cutting her off. "Bobby and I got married yesterday. I'm staying with him and the band."

"Married?" Her sister had always sworn she'd never marry, but now was no time to bring that up. "Now you can give Hailey a two-parent home," Lily reasoned. "A real family. Think of how wonderful that will be for the three of you."

"I don't want that. I never did."

"But—"

"Call me when you decide about Hailey." Without so much as a goodbye, Janice disconnected.

Numb with shock, Lily listened to the dial tone. She collapsed onto the lone stool in the booth.

Just as before, the sun was shining. Tourists were beginning to arrive. All around her, people were chatting and laughing. Everyone and everything looked so *normal*.

Only nothing was the same.

Janice was giving up her own daughter. She wanted Lily to raise Hailey. Dear God in heaven.

Wouldn't you know, several potential customers were making their way toward the booth. Too upset to care, Lily turned her back on them and called Selena. She asked her to hurry over and run the booth until Cindy arrived at seven.

That done, there was only one person Lily wanted to be with and talk to. Carter. He'd know what to do. Hoping he had time to see her, she dialed his office. "Hello, Linda. I need to see Carter right away."

"He's at lunch," Linda said.

"Can you tell me where?"

"At the Fisherman's Shack."

Which was walking distance from his office. "Is it a business lunch? Do you think he'd mind if I went over there?"

"He's alone, and I'm sure he'd enjoy seeing you. But he's been gone nearly an hour, and probably by the time you get there, he'll be back here."

"Is he booked all afternoon?"

"Pretty much. You sound funny. Is everything okay?"

"No," Lily said. "It's not."

"Anything I can do?"

Lily could tell that Linda was ready to listen and sympathize. But this was too new and complicated, and she felt too raw and emotional to go into it. "Just get me in to see Carter."

"Will do. I'll call him now and tell him you're on the way over."

CARTER WAS IN LINE at the Fisherman's Shack, waiting to pay his lunch bill, when his cell phone rang.

"It's Linda. Are you about finished with lunch?"

There was so much noise in the small café, he could barely hear his secretary. She didn't usually call during lunch. "Waiting to pay," he said over the hustle and bustle. "What's up?"

"Lily's on her way to the office. She sounded just awful."

"She did, huh?" It wasn't like Lily to leave her booth in the middle of the day, and he wondered if she'd somehow guessed that he didn't much like himself right now. Coward that he was. No, he was sure he'd hidden his feelings. At the front of the line now, he paid the cashier while still talking to Linda. "Did she say anything else?"

"Barely a word. Her voice was shaky, too, as if she was holding back tears."

Carter didn't like the sound of that. Was she having doubts about last night, about them? He sure as hell hoped not. "I'm leaving now." Mentally reviewing his afternoon, he pushed through the door. Several quarterly appointments, stuff that could keep for a few days… "Clear my calendar for the afternoon, will you?"

"I was thinking along those same lines. I'm on it."

Shortly after Carter returned to his office Lily rushed through the door. "I know we're supposed to see each other tonight, but this can't wait." She sank onto the chair across the desk. "I hope it's okay. Linda said it was."

"No problem. I rescheduled my appointments. Who's watching the booth?"

"Selena. She was glad for the extra hours." Lily swallowed visibly. She tugged off her bracelets. Put them on again. Chewed her lip and straightened the collar of her blouse, her eyes huge and filled with distress.

Carter had never seen her like this. Gut twisting, he leaned across his desk and took hold of her hands. "Lily, what's wrong? Is it about the IRS?"

She reclaimed her hands to hug herself. "Why, did they contact you? Oh, gosh, I can't handle any more bad news."

Bad news? "Haven't heard a word from them," Carter said. "Talk to me."

"Oh, Carter, the worst thing just happened. Janice called, and she's decided to give up Hailey!"

The anguished announcement caught him completely by surprise. "My God." He sank heavily against his chair.

"It's so upsetting." Her eyes flooded, her cheeks flushed red and she began to chew her poor bottom lip again.

Cripes, she was going to cry.

Carter jumped up, rounded his desk and pulled Lily to

her feet. He wrapped his arms around her. Trembling, she burrowed closer.

He kissed the top of her head. "I don't blame you for crying," he murmured, stroking her back. "Go ahead and let it out, honey."

Tensing and breaking away, she glared at him. "I'm not crying, I'm furious!" She began to pace the room. "I swear, if Janice were here, I'd strangle her! Doesn't she remember how rotten it feels to be abandoned by a parent?" She glanced over her shoulder at Carter. "Do you know what she said?"

Not about to get in her way or say a word, he shook his head.

"That if I don't take Hailey she'll turn her over to social services." Lily reached the window and pivoted toward him, her hair bouncing around her and her eyes flashing. "The gall!"

Carter had no trouble believing any of it. From the little he knew of Janice, she never had acted much like a parent. "It's pretty darned incredible," he agreed. "But not really a surprise."

"I guess not. Still…"

"I can't imagine," he said. "What are you planning to do?"

Never slowing, she shot him a how-can-you-even-ask look. "Raise her as my own, of course. If Janice doesn't care about Hailey, I do. I love her so much. I won't let this hurt her," she said, reminding him of a protective mother bear. "I'll adopt her, and she'll always know how much I love her. She's going to know the truth about Janice, too, and that none of this is Hailey's fault. The entire blame lies with my idiot sister. Ooh!"

Carter couldn't help comparing the situation with his own pitiful story. Did his daughter blame him for not seeing her? Did she think he'd rejected her? He'd never know, and there was no point wondering or suffering over it.

Chin high, Lily reached the bookcase. She spun around and marched toward him. "I know my hours are crazy and the houseboat is too small, but family is the most important thing in life. We'll make this work, especially when I get my hands on that building… I cannot fail the audit, Carter."

She looked fierce and determined. She was a fighter, and Carter admired her strength. He wanted to hold her again, but she seemed to need to move.

"You won't," he said. "Not if I can help it. And for the record, between you and Janice, you're the better mother. I think she knows that."

Some of Lily's bluster faded. Her face contorted, and Carter was sure she'd cry now. But she didn't.

"Want to hear something funny?" she said. "When she called and first asked me to keep Hailey a little longer, she actually said the same thing. I thought it was just talk, a way to get me to watch her daughter while she toured with the band. But now…" Lily rubbed her arms as if she was cold. "I wish I'd spent more time talking to her about it. Maybe I could've stopped Janice from making such a stupid, disastrous decision."

The person least at fault here was Lily. Guilt sucked, and hers was misplaced. "Don't you dare blame yourself for this," Carter said. "How many times have you tried to talk to her? She never returned your calls, and when she contacted you, she was always in a hurry to get off the phone."

"Thank you for reminding me, Carter. You're right, this isn't my fault."

The way Lily looked at him, as if he were her savior, made his chest hurt. He didn't deserve her trust, not until he told her about his daughter. And he would. But this definitely wasn't the right time.

"I still can't quite believe it." She stopped moving, blew the hair out of her eyes and sank against the wall. "Giving up your own flesh and blood—it's unnatural."

It was, but at least Janice herself had made the decision. Carter hadn't been lucky enough to get a say. Darla had taken his child someplace where he couldn't find her, leaving him in a hellish limbo.

"Hailey has you," he said, carefully masking his own agony. "That makes her a very lucky little girl."

"*Lucky* isn't a word I'd use for this situation. Regardless, here we are." Lily fished through her purse for a pad and pencil. "Do you happen to know of a good adoption lawyer?"

"No, but I do know several good attorneys. Sit down while I make a few calls."

AS THE SUN BEGAN TO SINK that evening, Carter sat in a redwood chair on his deck, eating the last of his Chinese takeout. It was good food, but sharing it would've been better. He wished Lily and Hailey were here, enjoying the beautiful evening with him. But Lily wanted to be alone. After what her sister had pulled today, that wasn't surprising. Lily had said she needed time to process and think.

Carter did, too. Since she had left his office this afternoon he'd thought about his daughter nonstop. His secret weighed heavier than ever on his shoulders, and he wished—

The phone rang, putting an end to his melancholy and regret. Eager to focus on something else, he snatched it up.

"It's me," his mother said. "Am I interrupting dinner?"

"Just finished."

"Good, because I need to vent. I can't believe Lily's sister decided to give up her own baby," she said, sounding as emotional as Lily.

"Yeah, it's pretty incredible."

"Really bad timing, too. Just when you were all set to tell her about your past."

"That'll have to wait."

"I have something to say about that later. First, I want to talk to you about Lily. When she picked up Hailey this afternoon… I've never seen her so distraught. She's a natural mother and obviously she adores that baby. Right now, Hailey's too little to understand what's happening, but what will she think later? Abandoned by her own mother for no good reason. Heaven only knows what that might do to her self-esteem…"

"You're thinking about your granddaughter, aren't you?" Carter said, scrubbing his hand over his face.

"I can't help it, son. This thing with Hailey brings it all back. When I picture our own flesh and blood, out there somewhere, a girl without a chance to get to know her father or her grandmother, and how that probably makes her feel… It hurts."

His mother sniffled, and Carter realized she was crying. He knew exactly how she felt. "Like a knife in the heart," he said.

They were both silent a moment, the pain between them a palpable thing. Then his mother blew her nose.

"Back to Lily. She really cares about you, Carter. I wish you'd heard her this afternoon, explaining how you got her the name of a good attorney in Anacortes, repeating the things you said to make her feel better. She lights up when she talks about you. I've seen you do the same when you mention her. You care a great deal about her, and that makes me very happy. Takes away some of the other pain."

"I know where you're going with this, Mom, but we haven't exactly talked about the future yet." Nothing beyond a brief mention of a long-term relationship. "So don't go jumping to any conclusions, and don't say anything to Lily or your friends."

"You have my word. I think you're smart to tell her about your past. If you're planning a future with her, she has the right to know. The sooner, the better."

Carter agreed. "Like I said, not now. She has enough on her plate." He couldn't drop a second bomb on her.

"That's where I disagree. I think you should go over there tonight and talk about it."

"She said she wanted to be alone."

"You and I both know she'd welcome your company. What's really stopping you, son?"

The cold fear that she might blame him for what had happened with his daughter. That she'd push him away. Carter wasn't about to admit that to his mother. "She's had a huge shock, Mom. She needs time to deal with that and get used to her new role in Hailey's life. I'll tell her after she meets with the attorney."

THE SATURDAY MORNING of Memorial Day weekend, Randi boarded the Greyhound with a duffel bag and backpack containing clothes, her wallet, iPod, phone and a stuffed koala bear she'd had since she was little. In other words, her most valuable possessions.

She'd never been so scared. But things at home were tense and she had no choice but to go. And the long weekend made this the perfect time.

Bright and early this morning, her mom and Richard had left Fort Dodge for a four-day vacation at Coralville Lake. They'd left Randi in charge of the house, and wouldn't be back until Wednesday. She'd written them a note, saying she was going to live with her father and wasn't ever coming back.

Randi doubted her mom would care. Richard would probably be thrilled.

She'd printed off Carter Boyle's office address and tucked it into the pocket of her jeans. Since his personal phone number and home address were unlisted, this was all she had.

She was finally going to meet him. A thought that made her stomach flip-flop. The first thing she would ask him was why had he written her off?

## Chapter Twelve

Traffic was terrible, and as Lily drove toward Carter's office after her meeting with the attorney Tuesday morning, she drummed her fingers on the steering wheel. It had been nearly a week since she'd met Carter at his office, and she was eager to see him.

Between work and Janice's decision, she'd needed time to herself. Carter had understood and had given her space. He'd been so sweet and supportive, calling to check in and make sure she was okay, that her misgivings that something was amiss had all but faded.

He'd invited her to lunch today. He wanted to know about her meeting with the attorney, and had asked her to come to the office.

Thanks to Selena, who was filling in at the booth, Lily was free the entire day. A good thing, since there was so much to tell Carter. Now that the adoption process was started, Lily no longer needed time to herself. She would invite Carter over tonight for dinner and cook something simple that she couldn't ruin. Then, once she put Hailey to bed, they'd make up for the days since they'd last made love. At the very thought her body hummed with anticipation. She could hardly wait to hold him, and be held.

Life was again looking up, and as Lily braked for a red light on Main Street, she thanked her lucky stars for her friends and employees who'd stepped in to help. Cindy and Selena at the booth, and dear, sweet Joyce, who was watching Hailey today while Henri had a doctor's appointment. And Charity. Only your best friend let you yammer on for hours at a time about the monumental changes in your life.

Lily owed them all so much. She had no idea how to pay them back, but she'd figure out something.

Just before noon she pulled into the parking lot at Carter's office. Right on time, too. Impatient to get to him, she hurried across the lot and pushed through the glass door.

"It's good to see you." Linda smiled. "How'd it go with the attorney?"

"There are lots of hoops to jump through before I can finally adopt Hailey, but that's okay," Lily said. "On the plus side, since I'm family the process won't be quite as difficult."

"That's something. If you need a character reference, holler."

"Thanks, Linda. You're the best."

"Ditto, kiddo." The secretary beamed and held up a large paper bag. "Your picnic lunch just arrived. Carter's expecting you. The way he's been acting this morning, antsy and tense, you'd think *he* was the one doing the adopting."

That he truly cared warmed Lily's heart. And she couldn't wait to see him. "A picnic. How sweet!"

"Tell Carter I'm going to lunch myself." Linda grabbed her purse from her desk drawer. "You two have fun. See you later."

Smiling, lunch in hand, Lily strode down the hall. The door was open. Carter was perched on the corner of his desk. His hair stood up in places, as if he'd absently combed it with his hand.

When he saw her, he stood and gave her a warm, intimate look that quickened her pulse. "You're finally here."

"Traffic wasn't great. Linda gave me this bag. She said to tell you she's gone to lunch."

Lily had barely set the bag on the desk before Carter pulled her into a hug. "It's good to hold you again."

Being nestled in his arms, pressed against his solid warmth, felt wonderful. "I've missed you so much," she said.

Standing on her toes, grasping his shoulders, she joyously participated in a long, tender kiss that left her breathless and wanting much more.

"Mmm, I like when you miss me." Carter gave her a slow grin that melted her heart.

"There's so much to tell you," Lily said.

"And I want to hear it all. There's a bench out back, perfect for a private picnic. Come on." Holding her hand and the lunch, he led her through the empty reception area and out the back door. In the midst of buildings a small grassy area had been fenced off, holding a lone tree. A wrought-iron bench under the spreading branches looked as if it were waiting for them.

Lily moved toward it. "It's nice out here. I didn't even know about this yard."

"Now you do. I don't get out here much myself, but I like the privacy. It's a good place to sit and think. And talk."

A muscle in his jaw ticced and he glanced away. The same funny feeling that something wasn't right filled the pit of Lily's stomach.

As if he'd read her mind, Carter gave a reassuring smile. Hadn't Linda said he'd been antsy all morning? Dismissing her worries, Lily sat down.

Carter joined her and handed her a sandwich and a pop. "Tell me about your meeting with the attorney," he said.

Ravenous, she unwrapped her sandwich and tore into it. "The lawyer contacted Janice and got her to agree to see a counselor," she related after swallowing a mouthful. "To make sure she really wants to do this. That will take some time. Then she'll have to sign some papers. For me, there'll be several home visits from a social worker." She hesitated.

"Are you worried about that?" Carter asked, toying with his pop. He hadn't touched his sandwich.

"A little. The houseboat is so small, and it's not exactly childproof. I suppose I could pack my jewelry supplies into the car. Or rent a storage space. But if I do either it'll be harder for me to make jewelry at night. And we'll still be crowded."

"What matters is that you love Hailey and she obviously feels the same way about you."

He was right. And who knew, if things continued to go well with her and Carter, maybe she'd move in with him. But it was too early in their relationship to be thinking about that. "You're in my life, I'm about to become a mom, and I'm being audited. A month ago, I could never have dreamed any of this. What a summer."

"You can say that again."

Lily waited for Carter to tell her he was glad they'd met, that he wanted to spend tonight with her. Instead, he pulled on the collar of his shirt and looked uncomfortable. He hadn't touched his sandwich yet, either.

Clearly his uneasiness had nothing to do with her visit to the attorney. Now she couldn't ignore her queasy stomach. She would find out what was bothering him, and this time nothing would get in the way.

"You're acting strange," she said. "And don't tell me nothing is wrong."

Carter turned to her. Swallowed. "You're right, there's something you should know, something I started to tell you at my place the other night."

Whatever it was, it made his shoulders rigid and his expression grim. Lily's uncertainties flooded back. Heaven only knew what he was about to say. But she trusted him, and whatever his problems, she would listen with an open mind. Together they'd figure out what to do. She offered an encouraging smile. "You can tell me anything."

"It's not easy to talk about." He laced his hands together and stared at the building's gray siding. "A long time ago, back when I was in high school, I—"

Abruptly, he broke off. Following his curious gaze, Lily saw a tall, pretty but rumpled-looking teenage girl carrying a duffel bag and backpack walk out the back door of the office. She moved hesitantly toward them. Something about her looked vaguely familiar, but Lily couldn't place her.

A good ten feet away, the girl stopped. "There's a sign out front that says everyone's at lunch. But the door wasn't locked, and I heard voices out here. I'm looking for Carter Boyle." She gripped the duffel with both hands, as if it were a life support. "That's you, right?"

"Guilty as charged." Carter frowned. "Do I know you?"

"You would if you'd ever bothered to meet me. I'm Miranda Gerrity—your daughter."

FEELING AS IF HE'D BEEN sucker punched, Carter gaped at the willowy girl before him. Miranda Gerrity—a name as unfamiliar to him as this teenager. The daughter he'd never imagined he'd have the good luck to meet was standing within feet of him. Eyes so like his own studied him, filled with the same pain and confusion he felt.

He didn't remember rising to his feet, but suddenly he had. "My God," he exclaimed. "It really is you."

"This is your— You have a daughter?" Lily asked.

The harsh, bruised sound of her voice ripped Carter's attention from his child. The color had drained from Lily's face. She stumbled to her feet.

And Carter knew that by keeping this very important information from her far too long, he'd wounded her deeply. Hating himself for what he'd done, he reached for Lily's hand. "Just let me—"

"Don't." Her eyes widening, she shrank back. As if touching him repulsed her. "I'll leave you two alone. Goodbye, Carter." Averting her gaze, she started for the office.

*Goodbye, Carter.* Such simple words that said so much. Carter's gut lurched. She couldn't leave, not like this. "Please, Lily, don't go. I can explain."

She glanced sharply at him but didn't reply. Didn't need to. The devastation shrouding her face spoke for her. *No explanation needed.*

As she hurried toward the back door, wrenching pain filled his chest. Torn between going after her and talking to his daughter for the first time, Carter turned to Miranda. "Stay right here," he said. "I'll be back."

He strode after Lily, who'd disappeared inside. When he rushed through the back door she was about to exit through the front.

"Wait," he called out.

Except for a momentary stiffening in her spine she gave

no sign that she heard him. He quickly closed the distance between them, then grasped her hand. It was ice-cold.

"Let go of me!" She jerked away and hurried out the door and into the parking lot.

On the sidewalk rimming the street beyond, pedestrians stopped to stare. Ignoring them, Carter kept pace with Lily. "If you'd just listen—"

Car key in hand, she spun toward him. "Why, so you can lie to me again? You have a daughter you never bothered to tell me about, a daughter you don't even know. You're no better than my own father!"

The accusation cut like a knife to the belly. Carter winced. "I wanted to tell you so many times. I was about to when she showed up. Believe me, I'm not at all like—"

"Don't waste your breath on me. Your daughter needs you. Go explain it all to her."

Lily's hand shook as she unlocked her car. Grim-lipped she slid into her seat, closed the door and revved the motor. Head high, attention riveted on the view through the windshield, she sped away.

Sick at heart, Carter watched her peel into the street. He wanted badly to go after her. But the way she'd looked at him… As if he were a snake or worse.

At the moment, he felt like one. He raked his hand through his hair and blew out a shaky breath. How many times had she asked, "Is anything wrong?"

He should've told her the truth a long time ago.

Because now he'd lost her trust and her love, and it hurt like hell.

Dammit, he couldn't let this happen. He wouldn't. He would straighten this out. He'd wait until Lily calmed down and was ready to hear his story. Hopefully, later tonight.

Right now, Miranda was waiting for him. Anxious to talk to his daughter, and at the same time feeling as if he'd aged a hundred years, he trudged toward the backyard.

UNCERTAIN WHERE TO BEGIN, Carter hung his thumbs in his belt loops, canted his hips against the tree and drank in the sight of his daughter. She was a beautiful girl, almost as tall as he was, and blond like her mother. He didn't much care for the long bangs brushing her eyes, or the tight jeans and belly shirt, though. She looked as if she hadn't bathed or changed her clothes in a while, either.

He glanced at the duffel and backpack she'd discarded, and wondered how she'd gotten here, where she'd come from. And if she planned on staying. Things he'd find out soon enough.

"I can't believe you're here," he said. "Why didn't you call?" If he'd known she was coming, he could've prevented this nightmare between him and Lily.

"Because this way, you couldn't hang up on me."

While he processed that horrendous statement, she flopped onto the bench. "Who was that woman who ran away, and why was she so upset?"

She was dead-on. Lily had run away, all right. "That's Lily. We're seeing each other." Carter hoped that was still true. "But let's talk about you. I spent years trying to find you, hoping you'd get in touch. Now you're here."

"I don't believe you." Her mouth an angry slash, Miranda crossed her arms over her chest. "My mom and grandparents said you were dead. If you wanted to see me, why would they lie like that?"

So that was the line they'd fed her—exactly the same crap Lily's mother had served up. A nasty lie that caused nothing but pain. And Carter hadn't been able to do squat about it. Which made him so damned mad. His hands curled into fists and he wanted to slug something. But losing his temper wouldn't help.

Forcing calm, he pressed his palms against the rough tree bark behind him. "Good question. I wish I knew the answer, but since your mother disappeared from my life over seventeen years ago, I'm at a loss here. What I *can* tell you is the truth. Darla and I went to high school together in Seattle. We'd been going steady two years when we found out she was pregnant." Carter recalled being scared but also awed that, together, they'd created a life. "Right away, I knew I wanted to get married and be a family."

Miranda looked skeptical. "Then why didn't you?"

"We were seventeen—your age. Too young for marriage, or so her parents said. I guess your mother agreed, because when I proposed, she turned me down and gave me back my class ring." Which, since he'd loved her, had broken his heart. "I had big plans to win her back. But no matter what happened between Darla and me, there was no doubt in my mind that I wanted to be a part of your life."

Miranda's mouth relaxed and opened slightly, and Carter saw that she was listening closely. He wanted to sit down beside her, but that might spook her. So he stayed put.

"The day you were born, the second I saw you and you looked at me with those big blue eyes…I fell in love. I couldn't wait to see you again. As soon as visiting hours started the next morning I rushed back to the hospital. But you and your mother were gone."

The agony of that moment was still with him, clogging his throat with emotion he didn't want to show. He glanced at the ground. "Your grandparents had taken you both away from me. My parents and I spent years and an enormous amount of money trying to find you. But your family changed their last name, and it was like you all had disappeared off the face of the planet. I never knew your first or last name until a few minutes ago."

All the years of emptiness, of not knowing. And now, finally… Unable to speak without embarrassing himself, he blew out a ragged breath and leaned heavily against the tree trunk.

His daughter stared at him through her thick bangs. "Is that true?"

Meeting her gaze straight-on, Carter nodded. "Every word. Not a day went by that I didn't think about you and wonder where you were, and what you were doing. I still carry the only picture I have of you." He fished his wallet from his pocket, extracted the creased, worn photo and handed it to her. "See?"

She studied it a moment, then silently handed it back.

"I wish things had been different," Carter continued, while Miranda picked at the polish on her thumbnail. "I wish I'd been there when you crawled and took your first step and celebrated your birthdays. For everything. I mean that, Miranda."

"Me, too." She brushed at her eyes, which now glistened with emotion. "Everyone calls me Randi."

Pretty emotional himself, he blinked hard. "Randi," he said, testing the name. "Tell me where you and your mom live. Are your grandparents well?"

"They used to live with us, but right after I turned sixteen, they were killed in a car accident."

"I'm sorry." Both because they were gone and because he wouldn't be able to confront them.

"Thanks. When they were alive, we moved around a lot. We were about to move to Fort Dodge, Iowa, when the accident happened. Mom already had a job lined up there with a pharmaceutical lab, so we moved anyway. That's where she met Richard, at work. They started dating. They got married in the fall, and we moved into his house." She made a face.

"You don't like Richard?"

"He doesn't like kids. Especially me."

Unsure whether she was telling the truth, and ready to protect her if need be, Carter shook his head. "How could anyone dislike you?" His daughter rolled her eyes. Because Carter had more questions he let it go for now. "When did you find out about me?" he asked.

"Mom and I don't get along anymore. A few weeks ago, we got into this huge fight. That's when she told me you were alive. She said that maybe I should go live with you. I thought she was making it up because she was mad. But then I looked you up online and found your Web site. And here I am." She gave a careless shrug, but her eyes were scared.

Fresh rage burned through Carter. At Darla for the lies, and what sounded like her jerk of a husband. For the seventeen years he'd lived without Randi in his life. "You must've been really upset."

Randi nodded. "I hate Richard, and I hate Mom!"

Not difficult to understand. "Exactly how did you get here?" he asked.

"Greyhound, Amtrak and the ferry. I missed the train and had to wait a whole day, so it took me four days."

That explained the unwashed look. "Does your mother know where you are? She must be worried sick."

His daughter shook her head. "They're at Richard's cottage on Coralville Lake and won't be back till tomorrow night. I have a cell phone, but so far Mom has only called once to check on me. They won't care that I'm gone. Besides, after keeping you and me apart all these years? She deserves to worry."

As furious as Carter was at Darla, he couldn't condone that. "You need to call her."

"Didn't you hear what I said? I'm really mad at her for lying about you! Besides, she doesn't care about me at all."

Were all teenage girls this dramatic? "Call anyway."

"Why don't *you* do it?"

Carter intended to. There was plenty he had to say to Darla, none of it for Randi's ears. For starters that if he wanted, he could have her arrested on kidnapping charges. "You call first. I'll talk later."

"Can I please do it tomorrow?"

"Today," Carter said. She looked so stricken that he added, "How about a compromise. You can wait until tonight."

"All right," she grumbled, grinding the toe of her sandal into the grass. She brushed the hair from her eyes. "Does this mean I can stay with you for a while?"

Carter liked the idea. He certainly had the room. But first there were things he needed to know. "Don't you have school?"

"There's only two more days before summer vacation. Finals were over last week, and now it's just a big waste of time. Most of the juniors and seniors skip."

He wished he could tell whether she was scamming him, but he knew next to nothing about teenagers. "You being straight with me?" he asked, narrowing his eyes.

"I swear."

She didn't flinch from his gaze, so he figured she was telling the truth.

"We'll see what your mom says. How're you doing in school? Are you getting good grades?"

"Okay. This semester, I should get an A and three B's."

"That's great."

"I guess."

"What's your favorite subject?"

"Algebra."

"I liked math, too."

"So that's where I got my math smarts. I always wondered."

He still couldn't believe his daughter was here, and they were talking about school as if she'd always been around. His mother would keel over when she found out. He was only sorry his father wasn't here.

"How would you like to meet my mom—your other grandma?" he asked.

"You mean she's still alive? What about your father?"

"Gone ten years now. He'd have been out of his mind with joy. And your grandma's right here on the island. Her name is Henri Boyle and she'll be so happy to finally meet you."

"Really?" Randi looked pleased. "Can we go see her right now?"

"She had a doctor's appointment, but she should be home by the time we get there. Come on."

Randi stood. "Dad?"

Hearing the name on her lips felt strange. And really good. "Yeah?"

Flushing, she ducked her head. "Would it be all right to give you a hug?"

"It sure would."

THE MORNING AFTER Carter's daughter arrived and Lily's world turned black, birds called cheerily to each other and the air was warm. Neither lifted her gloomy mood as she clutched Hailey and reluctantly knocked on Henri's door. She didn't want to be here, would've preferred never to see the woman again. But with no one else to watch Hailey yet, she had no choice but to bring the baby here.

Henri opened the door, her forced smile fooling no one. "Good morning, you two."

She swung the door wider and stepped aside so that Lily could enter. Too angry to go inside, Lily shook her head and stayed on the porch. Oblivious, innocent little Hailey laughed and reached for the older woman.

For some reason, the eager, loving expression on Henri's face made Lily want to sob. Anxious to leave before she did something foolish like break down, she handed over the baby. "I'll be back at the usual time," she said, looking everywhere but at Henri.

"Please don't go just yet. Won't you come in?"

"I'd rather not."

The older woman's face fell and she gave a resigned nod. "Carter must not have reached you last night. He was hoping to explain everything."

Oh, he'd definitely called, several times. Too distraught by his betrayal, Lily had ignored the phone. Later she'd erased his messages without bothering to listen to them.

Ending a relationship always hurt, but this had to be the most painful breakup of Lily's life. Pressure behind her eyes warned her that, like it or not, tears were coming. She would not cry in front of Henri.

But even as she blinked and fought for control, her eyes

filled. "Why didn't he tell me about Miranda, Henri? Why didn't you?"

Her sunny mood gone, Hailey made a sound of distress. She looked primed to cry, too. Obviously she'd picked up on Lily's emotional turmoil. *Darling, sweet girl.* For her sake, Lily attempted a smile. "It's okay, sweetie," she soothed. "I'm fine."

Not exactly the truth, but in time she would be. She always was.

Henri patted the baby's back and made tender, comforting sounds before again turning her somber eyes on Lily. "I only found out myself yesterday afternoon. After all these years, finally meeting Randi, hugging her... It's a true miracle—"

"I'm not talking about her showing up," Lily interrupted, angrily swiping her eyes. "You and Carter both know how deeply I value honesty." Lord knew, she'd talked about it often enough. "Knowing how I feel about Carter... How *could* you keep something this important from me?"

Even worse than that, Carter had neglected his daughter all these years. A man who seemed so moral and decent. He was good with Hailey, too. That Lily had been so blinded by her feelings she had ignored her persistent doubts sickened her.

Now Hailey was squirming. "She wants to be on the floor, so you may as well come in," Henri said.

Giving a terse nod, Lily stepped through the door. In the living room, Henri set Hailey down. Her toys were already out, and she scooted toward a tiny stuffed bear. Happy again, she cooed and hugged it. Henri gestured to a chair, but Lily remained standing. Unfortunately, the dam holding back her tears had broken, and they rolled down her cheeks.

Henri also remained on her feet, her own eyes wet. "I wanted to tell you about my granddaughter, but it wasn't my place. If it helps any, no one on the island knew about her, either."

What mattered to Lily was that Carter and Henri hadn't thought enough of her to tell her. She sniffled. "That doesn't help at all."

Now Henri was crying in earnest. Lily had never seen her so upset, and as the older woman pulled several tissues from the dispenser on the table, and handed her one, Lily actually felt sorry for her. Which just went to show how gullible she was. Foolish, foolish person. Her own tears stopped. Steeling herself against caring, against speaking, she clamped her jaw.

The words came anyway. "I told Carter *everything* about my past. He knew my parents lied, knew my father wanted nothing to do with me. And all this time, he was doing the same thing with his own daughter. So you can imagine how stupid I feel."

Why Henri looked confused was beyond Lily. She wasn't about to ask, since she no longer cared about either Henri or Carter.

The older woman blew her nose. "I'm not quite sure what you mean by that, but I do know that he planned to tell you about Randi. But then this crazy business happened with your sister. You were so distressed, and rightly so, that he decided to wait. I said to him, 'You tell Lily anyway,' but you know Carter."

Two days ago, Lily would've sworn that she knew him very well. Now her eyes were open and she realized she didn't know him at all. He had been right about one thing, though. They should've waited to get involved. If only they had, she might have been able to hold on to her heart.

Regardless, she didn't buy Henri's excuse. "Janice only told me she wanted to give up Hailey last week. Carter and I have known each other a lot longer than that. He had plenty of chances to tell me about Randi." How many times had she had asked, "Is anything wrong?"

The night they'd made love, they'd been as close as two people could get. Lily had given him her heart, bared her soul. And still he'd kept the fact that he had a daughter from her.

She was a fool for ever trusting him. First her mother and father, then Jerome, then her sister. Now Carter. The people you loved could not be trusted.

When would she ever learn?

Fuming at herself for being so darned gullible and thick-headed, she balled up the tissue and squeezed it hard.

"I'm truly sorry we hurt you, Lily," Henri said, dabbing at her eyes. "I just hope you'll find it in your heart to forgive us."

If Henri thought tears and an apology were enough to make Lily forgive and forget, she was wrong. Lily held her head high. "I trusted Carter and you. You both abused my trust. In my opinion, that's unforgivable."

"I see." Looking a dozen years older, Henri at last sank onto a chair. "I suppose you'll be wanting to get another sitter."

Hailey adored Henri and vice versa. Separating them would be painful for both, but it had to be done. "I e-mailed an ad to the paper last night," Lily said.

Henri gave a defeated nod. "At least let me watch her until you find someone else."

"I don't have much choice, do I?"

Until Lily hired a new sitter, the baby would come here. Lily would handle that by spending as little time as possible with Henri. And none with Carter.

Then she remembered. The audit. June nineteenth.

She needed him for that. Too bad it wasn't for another three weeks. No problem—from now on she'd only talk to him about matters relating to it.

Once the audit was over, she would never see him again.

## Chapter Thirteen

Dressed and ready for work Wednesday morning, Carter sat at the kitchen table blearily sipping coffee and waiting for Randi to wake up. He had no clue what she'd eat for breakfast. Whatever it was, he looked forward to this first breakfast with his daughter.

Who, he'd quickly realized yesterday, was exhausted from her long trek to Halo Island. After an emotional dinner with his mother, Carter had brought Randi home. During a quick tour of the house she'd chosen the room where Hailey had slept. Well before ten o'clock she'd showered and had fallen into bed. Carter hadn't heard a thing from her since.

As he drained his mug, his daughter padded barefoot into the kitchen. Her hair was in a lopsided ponytail and she wore a baggy T-shirt and pajama bottoms.

"Morning," he said, noting her bright eyes and rosy cheeks. "You look rested."

"I slept great." She slid into the chair across from him. "This is an awesome house."

"Awesome, huh. You want some cereal? Or I could scramble a few eggs."

"Cereal's fine."

"That's what I'll have, too." He stood, opened the cabinet adjacent to the sink and took down the two kinds he alternated between. "There's juice and milk in the fridge."

Moments later they were both seated at the kitchen table, eating cornflakes. Randi had drained a glass of OJ in seconds. She seemed ravenous, shoveling spoonfuls nonstop into her mouth.

When her bowl was empty, she wiped her lips with a napkin. "What'd my mom say when you talked to her?"

Thinking about that, Carter took his time chewing his mouthful. He wasn't about to repeat the conversation that had taken place after Randi went to bed. He'd yelled at Darla, and threatened to have her arrested for kidnapping. Not that he would. That would only hurt Randi, and she'd been through enough. But he'd wanted to scare Darla for putting him through hell. And he had.

After recovering from her surprise that Randi was with Carter, Darla had apologized profusely for keeping her from him all these years, had even turned on the waterworks. Her parents had pressured her to run away so that no one could take Randi from her. She'd been scared that Carter and his parents would try to do just that, she said. Carter wasn't sure he believed her and certainly didn't excuse her, but there was nothing to do but move on.

He swallowed his mouthful. "Same thing she told you," he said. "That you can live with me if you want."

Once he and Darla had moved past her apologies and talked about Randi herself, she'd actually sounded relieved that Carter wanted to take her. According to her, Randi was a handful and had been since her grandparents' death. Carter suspected that Darla's being wrapped up in her new husband hadn't helped.

"So I can stay with you for good?" Randi asked, look-ing hopeful.

"That'd be great." Carter had already missed so much time with her and didn't want to lose one more second. "If that's what you decide. Let's see how the summer goes."

"Okay, but I've already made up my mind. I'm staying." He yawned, and she looked at him. "You look tired."

"Yesterday was kind of a big day," he said. "Meeting you." And hurting Lily. "There was a lot on my mind, and I didn't sleep so well." For his sins he'd tossed and turned most of the night.

"I've been thinking about that woman—Lily," Randi said, as if she'd somehow read his mind. "She seemed so freaked out. Was that because of me?"

His daughter shrugged, a casual gesture that Carter had already come to realize hid her real feelings. She cared, all right.

How to explain what had upset Lily to a seventeen-year-old girl? But after yesterday, the one thing Carter knew for sure was that he was through dodging tough questions. "It wasn't your fault at all," he said. "It was mine. See, Lily shared everything about herself with me, even the ugly stuff. I led her to believe that I'd done the same. But that wasn't true. I left out a crucial part of my life. Even though you were always in my heart and my thoughts, I never told her about you."

Randi's eyes were wide with hurt. "Why not?"

The last thing Carter wanted was to cause his daughter further emotional pain. "I didn't tell anyone on the island," he explained, giving her a level look. "Talking about you when I had no idea where you were or if I'd ever see you— that just made me feel sadder and emptier. So I said nothing."

"I get that."

Randi's knowing nod assured him that she did indeed understand. Satisfied, he continued. "Lily grew up in a house where people told lies. Her mother lied about her father, the same way yours did. Only unlike me, her father approved of the lie. When Lily learned the truth, she found out where he lived and visited him. He refused to recognize her. He never has."

"That's lame!" Randi sounded truly outraged.

"Yeah. So you can understand why she values honesty above all else. When we started to get serious, I decided to tell her about you. Trouble was, I couldn't seem to find the right moment."

Now came the most sensitive part of the story. If Carter wasn't careful, Randi *would* blame herself for Lily's reaction. He sucked in a breath and blew it out. "I was finally on the verge of telling her when you walked into the backyard at the office. She was beyond shocked."

"Because she didn't know about me."

Feeling miserable, Carter nodded.

"You really like her, huh?"

"I'm crazy about her."

Elbow on the table and head propped in her hand, his daughter shook her head. "Jeez, Dad, you really screwed up. What are you going to do, buy her flowers?"

Carter almost smiled. "I don't think that'll cut it. I tried to get her on the phone last night." Wanting to make things right, he'd called three times. "She wouldn't pick up. I texted her, too. No reply." So he'd left messages, hoping she'd listen, and that she'd let him stop by. Having no idea how she'd feel about that, at one point he'd considered showing up on her doorstep and refusing to leave until he straightened out this mess. But after the way she'd looked at him when Randi had appeared.

Remembering that stunned, betrayed expression on her face, Carter cringed. Safer to stay away for a few more days. "We'll work it out," he said, determined to somehow make that true.

"You need to think of something bigger and better than a phone call or a text message."

Randi was right. Carter gave her a wry smile. "Thanks for the advice, Dr. Phil."

Missing the irony, she matter-of-factly brushed her bangs back. "Hey, why don't you take the day off and hang out with me? We can figure out what to do about Lily."

"Afraid I can't." When she looked downcast, he raised her chin. "It's only a few more days before the weekend. We'll spend Saturday and Sunday together."

She brightened. "That sounds great. Is it all right to have more cereal?"

"Eat as much as you want. This is your home, too."

"Thanks." She refilled her bowl and dug in.

His daughter ate as if she was half-starved. Carter recalled being the same way at her age. Mildly amused, he stifled a grin. And thought about the upcoming monthly poker game Saturday night at D.J.'s. He hated to miss it, but he'd just promised Randi the entire weekend. His friends would understand—once they got over their shock that he had a daughter.

He hoped they took the news better than Lily had.

"What am I supposed to do while you're gone today?" Randi asked.

"Why don't you come to work with me? Main Street happens to be filled with great shops, and the water's only a mile or so away. You can explore this morning. I'll take you to lunch, then you can look around some more." He recalled something Darla had mentioned. "You should probably get a job this summer."

"But I just got here! Do I have to?"

"It'll give you some spending money and something to do while I'm at work."

"I don't even know where to look."

"Tourist season is big here, and it's just starting. Everyone's hiring. Maybe you'll find something near my office."

EVEN THOUGH SOME of the towns Randi had lived in were bigger than Halo Island, Main Street was filled with more people than she'd ever seen. You could tell they were tourists by the way they gawked at everything. There were girls her age and more than a few cute guys, most of them hanging out with their parents. One or two caught her eye and smiled. Blushing, Randi looked away.

Wanting everyone to think she was a local—after all, she lived here now—she did her best to look relaxed and comfortable, like she knew what was what. But with all the awesome shops and the huge, pretty hanging flower baskets, pretending she was totally at home wasn't easy.

Halo Island was so cool. For one thing, there were seagulls everywhere. And the sun was so bright the air was almost blue. And no matter where she went she smelled the ocean.

She couldn't see it from Main Street and wasn't sure exactly where it was, but her dad had said it was nearby. If she asked, she knew she'd find out. But she wasn't about to do that. Then people would know she was new here.

Feeling very grown-up, she wandered in and out of several shops—a women's clothing store with stuff too old for her, a music store and a cool bookstore with lots of books and magazines she wanted to read. The bookstore wasn't hiring, but the music store said they might be. She stopped at a cute little café several blocks from her dad's office and asked for a job application. Who knew, maybe her dad would bring her here for lunch.

It was so great to finally meet him and find out that he cared about her. Randi was really happy that she'd come.

A soft breeze ruffled her hair, bringing with it the strongest scent of ocean yet. With that, she made up her mind. She was supposed to be back at her dad's office when the noon bells rang, which wasn't for a while yet. She'd find the ocean, maybe wade through the waves. Too bad she hadn't brought her swimsuit this morning. She'd left it at her dad's house.

As she reached the next corner, where Front Street intersected Main, she finally saw the water. It was only a few blocks away, at the end of Front Street. But what snagged her attention were the group of what looked like huts right across the street.

There were a whole bunch of them and tons of people milling around, shopping. Colorful, artsy-looking items hung from some of the booths. Intrigued, Randi decided to look around there and save the ocean for later.

Liking the handmade crafts and the cool-looking people who made and sold them, she picked up several job applications. At a booth with the sign Halo Island Carver, Brett, who sculpted birds and whales out of black stone, asked her to come back for an interview later that afternoon. Randi was totally excited. It would be so awesome working here.

She noticed a big crowd of women in front of one of the huts looking at jewelry. Randi loved beaded earrings and necklaces, and started toward them. Then she noticed the person working behind the counter.

It was that woman her dad liked. Lily.

Uncertain whether to show herself or not, Randi hung back, watching. Lily seemed warm and friendly, and smiled a lot—not at all like yesterday. But when the shoppers left and she was alone, her smile faded and she looked really sad. The way Randi had felt when her mom started paying attention to Richard and ignoring her.

Lily probably looked that way because she was fighting with Randi's dad. If they liked each other, they ought to make up and be happy, unless Lily was like Richard and hated kids. Randi wasn't sure.

If she got a job here and worked close to Lily, maybe she'd get to know her a little and find out.

The noon bells began to chime, meaning she was late. Now she'd have to run to get back. Randi did just that.

"SURE YOU DON'T WANT TO go to bunco?" Charity asked as she joined Lily and Hailey on the love seat in Lily's living room. "I know you don't have a sitter, but you took Hailey with you last time and really enjoyed yourself."

That was where Henri had first offered to babysit. Had it only been a month? So much had happened that it seemed a lifetime ago.

Lily shook her head. "I don't feel like it."

"But you love bunco. You've never missed a game." Charity eyed her. "Don't tell me it's because Henri will be there? You live in a small town, so you'd best get used to running into her."

"It's bad enough seeing her every time I drop Hailey off and pick her up." Lily had yet to find a replacement sitter. "Besides, by now everyone in town knows about Randi. The room will be abuzz with talk about her, and I can't handle that." She was still too mad at Carter.

"You know that Brett Harmon just hired her to work at the Halo Island Carver booth. She starts Monday."

"So I heard." Lily didn't know what to make of that. Except that Randi must be staying in town for the summer. Lily certainly hadn't asked Henri about it. She hadn't spoken more than two words to the woman since Randi had shown up. That Carter hadn't sent his daughter home again meant that he was finally willing to get to know her—a mark in his favor.

"You're not planning to give her the cold shoulder, too, are you?"

"Or course not." It was getting close to Hailey's bedtime, so Lily tugged off the baby's socks. Randi was an innocent, a child her father hadn't recognized—until she'd forced him to. "None of this is her fault."

In no mood to discuss the matter further, Lily steered the conversation to a more neutral topic. "Back to bunco. You missed last month's game, so if you want to go tonight, please do. You don't have to hang around here for my sake. I'm pretty bad company tonight, and you'll probably have a lot more fun there."

"You're my best friend, and you stuck by me when Trevor broke my heart. Plus we're both working so much, we hardly ever get to see each other. I want to spend time with you." Charity fished through her purse. "I rented a couple of your favorite classic movies for after Hailey goes to bed. *Casablanca* and *It Happened One Night*. They're sure to take your mind off your troubles."

"That's great." As Lily unhooked Hailey's bib overalls, her eyes filled. "Sometimes I think that you and Hailey are the only people in the world I can trust."

"What about Joyce and Cindy? And that girl you hired, Selena? And Carter's secretary, Linda?"

All women Lily liked and considered friends. "I guess I can trust them."

Charity nodded. "Now don't get mad, but in my opinion, you can trust Henri, too. And Carter."

Lily's jaw dropped. "After what he did? No way. And his mother's just as bad."

"I get that he should've told you about his daughter. Okay, the man made a mistake. Who hasn't? I say cut him some slack. And quit blaming Henri. She adores Hailey and she likes you, too. Besides, it wasn't her responsibility to tell you anything."

Henri had said the same thing. Lily didn't buy the excuse and couldn't believe what came out of her friend's mouth.

"Whose side are you on?" she asked, carefully pulling Hailey's shirt over her head. "It's not just that he didn't tell me about something so important. Don't you see that? The way he treated Randi, or should I say *ignored* her, makes him no better than my own father." Lily felt genuinely sorry for the girl. "Knowing that, how could I ever be with him?"

"There are several reasons. Number one, you love him."

"I've fallen in love before," Lily said, laying Hailey on her back. "I'm a big girl and I'll get through this." She nuzzled the baby's round little belly and earned a delighted squeal. "Won't I, sweetie?"

"Reason number two, I'm not at all sure you have the story right."

"What do you mean?" Lily frowned as she changed Hailey's diaper.

"You said it yourself often enough—Carter Boyle is a good man. I'm thinking there's more to this whole thing than you know. If it were me, I'd give him a chance to explain."

"I can't believe you! I was there, and I heard and saw everything. Carter didn't even know his own daughter. She had to tell him who she was. That's the story, and the subject's closed."

"But—"

"But nothing. I don't want to think about Carter or Henri anymore tonight." Lily guided Hailey's arms and legs into her pajamas and zipped them up. "I'm going to put Hailey to bed, and when I come back we're going to watch those movies. Period."

Charity sighed. "If that's the way you want it, fine. But for the record, I think you're wrong."

CARTER SAT AT HIS DESK, supposedly reviewing a business client's assets and liabilities. But with his own personal assets and liabilities to mull over, he couldn't concentrate. Newest on the asset side was Randi. He smiled. Getting to know her was so wonderful, even if she could be moody and dramatic. According to Linda, who'd raised five kids, all teenagers were like that.

Randi seemed to be settling in well, liked her job and had made a few friends. Best of all, she hadn't changed her mind. She wanted to stay with him and finish high school on the island.

While that was great, the liability side sucked. Lily was still avoiding him. It had been two whole weeks since he'd seen or spoken to her. He missed her. Missed her warmth, missed holding her and hearing about her day. He missed Hailey, too.

Back to the assets. At least Lily didn't hold his short-comings against Randi. According to his daughter, since she started her job, she and Lily had eaten lunch together once or twice. They'd talked about jewelry, work, Hailey, and Randi's developing relationship with Carter. Randi liked Lily. She thought Carter should make things right again.

The whole town seemed to know about his and Lily's troubles and agreed with Randi. Linda, Alex, D.J., Ryan and their wives were all on his case. Carter's mother, who was still watching Hailey, also hated that Lily was so tense and aloof.

Carter wished he could get her to listen. She wouldn't take his calls, refused to answer her door when he knocked, and probably deleted every one of his text messages and e-mails. Last week he'd even taken Randi's advice and sent flowers. Which hadn't done a thing, he'd learned when he'd stopped by Lily's booth the following day. She'd been so cold and distant she'd given him frostbite.

Carter winced. Luckily, his daughter hadn't witnessed that. Randi had had a day off and was at the beach with friends.

What was a guy to do? Hell. He scrubbed his hand over his face. Maybe he'd—

Linda buzzed, interrupting his sorry thoughts. "Tom Bigelow is on line one."

Owner of an ice cream franchise and a Laundromat, Bigelow was a long-standing client. And a windbag. In no mood for a twenty-minute monologue, Carter scowled at the intercom. "Tell him I'm too busy for his bull."

"I will not," Linda said. "I'll say you stepped out. Since you're in such a bad mood, maybe you ought to do just that."

"Fine. I will." Carter disconnected. Hands in his pockets, he wandered toward the reception area. "I'll be back later," he grumbled.

His secretary gave him a curious look, but when he narrowed his eyes in warning, she wisely kept her mouth shut.

Fifteen minutes later, without having planned it, he stood on the sidewalk across the street from the booths, squinting in the bright sunlight and wishing he'd thought to bring his shades. As usual, the place was thick with tourists.

Now that he was here, he'd say hello to Randi. He made his way through the crowd. Busy with customers, his daughter greeted him with surprise. "Dad. What are you doing here in the middle of a workday?"

Not sure himself, Carter kicked the dirt. "Needed some air," he said.

He couldn't help glancing toward Lily's booth. May as well try again to talk to her.

"Ah." His daughter crossed her fingers. "Good luck."

## Chapter Fourteen

Having selected three sets of earrings, necklaces and bracelets, Lily's fortysomething customer smiled happily and handed over the money. "My daughters will love these."

"You picked some nice pieces," Lily said.

As she wrapped the purchases, she sensed that someone was watching her. She looked past her customer, and sure enough, someone was. Carter. He was striding toward her, the startling blue of his eyes noticeable even from a distance.

This was the second time in a week that he'd come. Would he never learn? Lily frowned. She was through with him. Yet even as she reminded herself, her breath caught and her heart lifted in anticipation.

"Are you all right?" her customer asked, glancing over her shoulder. She must've noted Carter's intent gaze, for she raised her eyebrows. "No wonder you're distracted. He's very good-looking, and he's obviously on his way to see you."

"Well, he's wasting his time." Lily jerked her gaze from Carter.

"By the determined look on his face, he doesn't think

so. He must've done or said something awful to upset you like this."

"And then some," Lily muttered, beyond caring that this virtual stranger could read her so well. Refusing to so much as glance again at Carter, she offered her best customer-friendly smile. "Thanks for your business, and please come back. If you'd like to order again, all my designs are posted on my Web site. I'll stick three business cards in the bag."

"Here he comes," the woman said. "Good luck."

She left and Carter took her place. Big and handsome, he rested his forearms on the counter, claiming the entire space so that no one else could. "Hello, Lily," he said soberly.

"You're here again." Fighting the urge to reach out and touch his face, Lily backed up a step. She gestured toward an earring display on the back wall. "If you're looking for something for Randi, these are popular with teenage girls."

"I'll keep that in mind, but that's not why I'm here. This cold-shoulder business has gone on long enough. We *are* going to talk."

How many times had she heard him say the same words, only to shuffle around—no, plain-out evade—the truth? "Unless this is about the audit, there's nothing to say," she replied, proud of her indifferent tone. "Not that I want to hear."

Carter stiffened. Eyes flashing, voice raised, he swore. "Dammit, Lily. If you'd just listen—"

If she hadn't known him so well, his forbidding expression would have intimidated her. It actually did, a little. Trembling slightly, she managed to look down her nose at him. "People are staring. Please keep your voice down."

He opened his mouth, but she cut him off. "Why can't you just go away and leave me alone?"

"Is that what you really want?"

"Yes."

His eyes narrowed a fraction before he exhaled loudly. "All right, I won't pressure you anymore. From now on, we're client and accountant, period. But if I'm representing you in your upcoming audit, which happens to be one week from today, we'd damn well better communicate about it."

This she could do. "As I just said, if you want to discuss the audit, talk away."

Carter gave a curt nod. "Michael Woods has scheduled our meeting for ten-thirty, in a building across town. We should plan to arrive early, but first, we need to meet and discuss strategy. I'll expect you in my office at nine sharp."

"I'll be there." Selena had already agreed to work that day. "How long do you think the audit will last?"

"Couple of hours. I assume Woods has already checked your Web site. He'll probably want to see this booth and look at your inventory."

Lily felt Carter's emotional withdrawal as keenly as she felt the hard floor beneath her feet. Suddenly it was as if they were strangers and had never discussed anything personal, never shared dizzying kisses or made passionate love.

It was best this way, and what she told herself she wanted, but her heart disagreed. The gash in it gaped wider.

She swallowed around the icy lump in her throat. "I'll be ready."

THE DAY OF THE AUDIT Carter stared out his office window while he waited for Lily. Wouldn't you know, it was rainy this morning, and as dark and gloomy as a winter day. Or his soul, now that he'd lost her.

That last time at her booth he'd really studied her eyes

and listened to her, and the truth had finally penetrated his thick skull. Lily no longer loved him. Once, she'd mouthed the words and acted as if she cared, but he now realized she'd confused passion with love.

A painful but apt lesson. It didn't pay to get involved with a client. If he'd stuck to the damned rule he wouldn't be feeling so beat-up. Regardless, he was a good CPA, and even if his love life was in the crapper, he'd do everything possible to pass the audit.

Right on time, Linda buzzed that Lily was here.

Seconds later she entered his office. Her cheeks were pink, and the scent of fresh, wet air clung to her. Carter had never seen a more beautiful woman. Steeling himself against an onslaught of feelings, he greeted her with a nod. The raindrops glistening in her hair did not draw his attention, and neither did the striped aqua dress that clung to her curves.

But the tension radiating from her was impossible to ignore. She was nervous about the audit, he figured. That was enough to put anyone on edge.

As Carter moved to the desk and gestured for her to sit down, she straightened her bracelets.

"You're wearing a jacket and tie. You didn't tell me to dress up."

"You look fine," he said, keeping his eyes on the space over her shoulder. "Now, we don't have much time, so let's get started. Here's how it should go. Michael Woods will start with questions. Then he'll ask to see the booth, and probably ask more questions. Then we'll go back to the audit room for one more round of questions."

"What will he ask me?"

"About the worktable your ex made you, for starters. And the other things we went over before. We don't want to miss supplying the IRS with whatever records and information they want, so I'll be taking notes."

"Should I do that, too?"

He shook his head. "Your job is to honestly answer any question Woods asks. Answer only the question. Don't give him any other information."

She shot him a quizzical look. "Why not?"

"Trust me, this is the way it's done."

She looked at him as if she'd never trust him again.

Nothing new there, but he still felt lower than pond scum. He wanted to howl in frustration. But they were about to go into an audit, and this was not the time to lose his cool.

Carter squeezed the bridge of his nose and reined in his feelings. "Listen, I've handled plenty of audits, and in my experience, it's best if the client says as little as possible. Like they do in court. So you don't incriminate yourself."

"But I have nothing to hide."

He squinted at her. "Look, do you want to win this audit or not?"

"Of course I do." She pushed her hair back, squared her shoulders and regarded him with those caramel-colored eyes.

It was the first time in ages that she'd actually looked at him. For one long moment, Carter lost himself in those liquid depths. A big mistake that would get him exactly nowhere. He returned his gaze to the space over her shoulder. "If I think you're saying too much, I'll pull on my ear, like so."

As he demonstrated, a smile tugged her lips. "Got it," she said.

For one brief moment she looked like the Lily he used to know, the woman who cared for and trusted him. But that woman was gone. His chest aching, he reviewed other points with her. Then it was time to head out.

"You ready?" he asked, pushing back his chair and rising.

"Not really." She stood and smoothed her dress. "I'm scared. So much is at stake."

It was all he could do to keep from pulling her into a reassuring hug. "Trus— I'll give it my best shot. Let's go do this."

MICHAEL WOODS, the IRS auditor, looked exactly as Lily had pictured him—reedy, thin and balding, with a no-nonsense expression. He perched primly at the head of a rectangular table in a small conference room the IRS had rented for the audit. Lily and Carter sat on either side of him, across from each other.

"Tell me about this carpentry expense," he said.

Carter tensed—nothing you'd notice unless you knew him as well as Lily did. He was apprehensive about this.

She was scared half to death. Her mouth went dry and she sipped from the bottle of water Carter had thoughtfully provided. "Some of it was for repairs to the booth where I sell my jewelry during the tourist season," she said. "But most of it was for a worktable that was custom-designed for me."

"We have photos and supporting documents," Carter said. He slid copies toward Mr. Woods.

For a few moments the auditor was silent, studying the information while tapping a mechanical pencil against his narrow lips. "I'd like to see the table myself," he said.

"The thing is, I don't have it anymore. It's too big for my tiny houseboat. If you saw my house, you'd know that just about everything is, and—"

Carter pulled on his earlobe and she stopped chattering.

"Lily still owns the table," Carter said. "But one of her employees uses it at her home."

Lily nodded. "If you want, I could call her and ask if we—"

Carter pulled his ear again, and she went silent. She always talked too much when she was nervous.

Bent over his spiral notebook, Michael Woods didn't seem to notice. He was too busy scribbling notes.

He looked as if he'd just sucked on a very sour lemon. He must be thinking the worst, that she'd deliberately tried to cheat the IRS. But she hadn't! Lily's stomach wrenched, and she thought she might throw up.

She started to hug her waist, but didn't want Mr. Woods to know how scared she was. So she placed her hands together as if in prayer and touched her fingers to her lips. Carter almost smiled at that, something he wouldn't do if he thought things were going badly. Her spirits lifted a tiny bit.

At last the auditor set down his pencil and closed his notebook. "I'd like to see your primary place of business. My car's out front."

"Is it okay to tell Selena, my part-time summer help, that we're on the way?"

He nodded. "Certainly. I'll just use the facilities and meet you out front."

Lily made a quick call to Selena. It had stopped raining, so she and Carter waited for the auditor outside. The sun was shining again, and everything smelled fresh and clean.

"You're doing a good job," he said.

"Except I keep talking too much. All that pulling on your ear—it must be pretty sore."

"Nah. I'd say it's going well so far."

"How can you tell?"

"Woods isn't asking the nitpicky questions I expected."

"But he still could."

Carter shrugged. "You never know."

As warm as it was outside, Lily shivered. "I've never been so terrified."

"Hang in there." Carter reached out to her, hesitated and pulled his hand back.

Lily wished things were different. She needed his reassuring touch.

Michael Woods exited the building and strode toward them. "Shall we go?" He led them to his black sedan.

A short time later they parked on Front Street and headed for the booth. On the way, they passed the Halo Island Carver, where Randi worked. Eyes widening, she looked from Lily to Carter as if trying to figure out whether anything had changed between them. When she made a face at Mr. Woods's back, Lily guessed Carter had told her about the audit.

Everyone knew and as Lily passed by, several business owners held up crossed fingers.

An hour later, after a dozen questions, which Lily answered, Mr. Woods drove them back to the conference room. Just as Carter had predicted, more questions followed.

She replied to each one, trying not to supply any extra information. When she did, Carter continued to tug his ear. Often he added to her answer. The whole thing would've been exhausting if she weren't so hyped up with worry.

When it ended at last, nearly four hours later, she felt completely wrung out, but relieved that it was finally over.

If Carter was tired, he didn't show it. "I'll fax or e-mail you the information you requested within twenty-four hours," he said, shaking Mr. Woods's hand.

Lily shook it, too.

The auditor made a last notation in his notebook, then nodded. "I'll be in touch."

"What happens now?" she asked as he drove away.

"We send the IRS the documents they want. Then we wait."

"For how long?"

"I can't say for sure—about a week or two. First Woods will contact me. Then the IRS will send a letter. When I hear something, I'll be in touch."

Lily knew she ought to get to the booth so Selena could go home, but she needed time to regain her energy. If things were different, she'd have invited Carter to join her for a late lunch. Or maybe they'd relax in a totally different, far more pleasurable way.

But all that was behind them now. Once Carter heard from Mr. Woods, Lily would never see or talk to him again. It was what she wanted, and nothing had ever hurt so much.

Hiding her pain, she offered her hand. "Thank you, Carter."

"Pleasure." His handshake was firm and all too brief. Just as it should be between a CPA and his client.

THE ALARM WENT OFF far too early, especially after a bad night's sleep. Groaning, Lily shut it off. The anxieties that were with her all the time flooded her mind, and instantly she was wide-awake. It was Friday, the tenth day after her grueling audit. Carter had said it wouldn't be long before they heard from Mr. Woods and the IRS.

Would today be the day she'd find out whether she lost everything?

As frightening as the thought was, Lily preferred knowing to this endless waiting. She was sick of having knots in her stomach.

And Hailey would soon wake up. With no time to waste, and feeling too uptight to lie in bed anyway, Lily rose. She put on the coffee, though she was so tense she probably didn't need it, then hastily stepped into the shower.

She wished she could talk to Carter. She needed his reassurance. Needed him, period.

But true to his word, he'd left her alone. Which was what she'd assured him she wanted. Yet she missed him terribly. She was certain Hailey did, too.

"Maybe he'll hear from Mr. Woods and call today," she murmured as she washed her hair. It was pitiful how much she looked forward to hearing from Carter.

And not so easy pretending she was fine around Randi and Henri, either. Lily saw them both nearly every day. The more she knew Randi, the more she liked the girl.

As for Henri… Keeping her distance from Carter's mother was no fun at all. Standing under the spray, Lily let out a sigh. While tossing and turning last night, she'd actually considered forgiving and forgetting. But she had her principles and meant to stick by them—even if it meant loneliness. With fresh determination, she shut off the shower.

The one bright spot in her life was Hailey. The baby's love and sweet laughter lightened Lily's burdens and filled her heart. Already she thought of the little girl as her own.

She was spooning warm cereal into Hailey's eager mouth when the phone rang. Not wanting to disrupt breakfast, Lily set the phone on speaker. It was the adoption attorney.

"I just heard from Janice's counselor," he said. "The counseling sessions are over. Your sister hasn't changed her mind. She still wants to give up her baby."

Had Hailey understood that? Alarmed, Lily glanced at the little girl. She seemed intent only on her food.

"That's great news," Lily said. "I mean…you know what I'm saying."

"I'm happy for you, Lily. A social worker will be in touch later this week."

Lily glanced around her much tidier kitchen. By staying up and working into the night a few times, she'd managed to transfer most of the jewelry supplies to her car. Given that she needed to keep busy every second so that she didn't moon about Carter, she was almost glad for the extra work.

"I'm ready," she said.

Bursting with the news, she buckled Hailey into her car seat and headed for Henri's. This was something she could share with the older woman, who would want to know. Henri would tell Carter, too.

When Lily knocked on the door, Randi answered.

Lily knew she looked surprised. "I didn't expect to see you here."

"Friday is my day off. My friends are busy, and since my dad doesn't like me to be alone all day… You know parents." Randi rolled her eyes, then grinned as if she liked it that her father cared. "Grandma's going to teach me her secret brownie recipe. She says I can help take care of Hailey, too. Is that okay?"

"Of course." Remembering her own baking lesson and how close she'd felt to Henri that day, Lily felt a pang of remorse. Which, given what had happened, was ridiculous. "Your grandma's a good teacher," she said. She set Hailey on the living-room floor. "Where is she?"

"In the bathroom. She'll be out in a minute."

Meaning Lily could leave without seeing her. She would have, only she wanted to share the news. "I'll wait, then. I need to talk to her."

"You do?"

Randi's expressive eyes widened, and Lily realized she knew everything. For some reason this embarrassed her. "It's about Hailey," she said, needing to clarify. "Something your grandma will want to know."

"Okay. Do you want to sit down or something?"

Lily shook her head.

Randi flopped on the floor beside Hailey and ruffled her hair. The baby jabbered and smiled.

"What's an audit like?" Randi asked.

"Draining. The auditor asks tons of questions and you have to answer them all. But you have no idea if he likes your answers. Then you have to wait *forever* to find out how you did."

"Like you're waiting now."

"Right."

Randi's forehead creased. "If you're the one answering the questions, what does my dad do?"

"Makes sure the person being audited is prepared, and helps when you get off track. At least he did for me," Lily said. "He's great at it, too." And at so many other things too private to share.

"I figured he was." Clearly proud of her father, Randi beamed.

Curious, Lily asked a question that had been on her mind for some time. "You're not upset with him for not seeing you all these years?"

"I was, but not anymore. I know he loves me and he's glad I'm here. He's the best dad ever." Randi let out an adult-size sigh. "I just wish he was happy." She gave Lily a sly look that reminded her of Henri. "He would be if you'd give him a chance."

Lily said nothing. Then again…if Randi could forgive him, maybe she should, too. She'd at least think about it.

At last Henri entered the room, stopping on the threshold when she spied Lily.

"Grandma, Lily has something to tell you."

"Oh." Henri looked surprised, but all she said was, "If I'd known, I would have come out sooner. I hope you don't mind if Randi helps today."

"I think it's great," Lily said. "I'm sure Hailey will love all the added attention." She glanced at the baby, happy on the floor.

"What did you want to say?" Henri asked.

It had been so long since Lily had actually spoken to her. Feeling awkward, she hesitated, but the woman's encouraging nod eased some of the tension.

After darting a quick glance at Hailey, Lily lowered her voice. "I heard from the adoption attorney this morning. Janice has finished her counseling and we're ready to proceed with the adoption."

"I'm so happy for you." Henri smiled with genuine joy. "And for Hailey."

"Me, too," Randi said. "Both my grandma and my dad say you're a really good mom."

"I'm trying. Thanks."

The warmth and love on Henri's face were hard to miss. Despite Lily's chilly behavior toward her, she still cared.

Filled with remorse for the way she'd treated the older woman, Lily opened her mouth to apologize. *What about your principles?* a voice in her head asked.

Swallowing her words, she turned away. "I should go now. I'll be back at the usual time."

"GIVE MY DAD A CHANCE," Randi had urged. It was the same thing Lily had thought about for hours while tossing and turning last night. Throughout the morning, as she helped various customers, she seriously considered doing just that.

As her accountant, Carter had worked hard for her. As her lover, he'd shown her passion and joy. Hiding the fact that he had a child from her had cut her deeply. But what could it hurt to hear what he had to say? *If* he still wanted to explain. After all this time, he might have changed his mind.

Randi could be mistaken. Carter might not want Lily anymore.

A possibility that had her swallowing hard. Regardless, he deserved a chance to explain. Lily was ready to give him that chance.

Now that she'd made up her mind, she was anxious to see him. But it was just after two. Cindy wasn't due until seven.

Lily called Selena and asked if she could come in, but she was busy.

Next she tried Cindy. Lily updated her friend about the adoption before explaining the real purpose of her call. "I need to see Carter, and Selena can't work. Is there any possibility that you could come in early?"

"You heard from the IRS." Cindy sounded breathless.

"Not yet."

"Did you and Carter make up?"

"That depends on what happens when we talk."

"Why didn't you say so? I'll be there by four."

Lily let out a relieved breath. "Thanks, Cindy. You're a lifesaver."

As busy as the day was, the time seemed to crawl by.

When Cindy finally showed up, Lily grabbed her purse. "Wish me luck."

"Good luck." Her friend hugged her.

As Lily wove between throngs of tourists to reach Main Street, she saw Carter striding toward her. Heart lifting, she hurried to meet him.

"Where are you headed?" he asked, looking surprised to see her.

"I was on my way to find you."

"You were?" His eyebrows rose quizzically. "Funny, I'm on my way to see you. We must have ESP."

He must've heard from the IRS. Forgetting for a moment what she wanted to say, Lily bit her lip. "You heard from Michael Woods."

Carter nodded. "And it's pretty good news. The IRS dismissed most of their case against you. They reduced what you owe by ninety percent."

"Yippee!" Lily pumped both fists into the air. Several pedestrians eyed her and veered away, but she didn't care.

"You still have to pay," Carter warned.

Her stomach did its knot thing, and Lily hugged herself. "How much?"

"With interest and penalties, a big chunk of money— so brace yourself."

He gave her the dollar amount, which was four figures. It *was* a lot of money, but wouldn't wipe her out.

"That's a whole lot less than it was." With this year's sales so strong and sure to continue, by September she'd easily have the rest of the down payment for Mr. Creech's building.

"Without your help…I'm so grateful to you," Lily exclaimed. Unable to suppress her relief, she threw her arms around Carter.

He stiffened and she let go. And knew with sickening certainty that she'd indeed waited too long, that Carter had changed his mind. He no longer cared.

"I'm sorry," she said, feeling empty inside. "I had no right to do that."

"You tell me to leave you alone, and now you hug me." His expression was guarded. "I don't get it."

Even if he no longer had feelings for her, she owed him an explanation. "I was on my way to see you because…I've been thinking, and I know I haven't been fair. If you still want to explain about Randi, I'm ready to listen."

Chin angled, he studied her. "You are?"

Lily nodded. "I want to know everything. But if you don't want to tell me, I totally understand."

"There's nothing I want more. Let's go someplace and talk right now."

"How about the backyard of your office?" Where everything had unraveled.

On the walk there, neither of them spoke. Lily's heart pounded so loudly she wondered if Carter could hear it. He was so quiet. If only she knew what he was thinking.

Linda had gone home early and had closed up for the day, so Carter unlocked the front door and ushered Lily through. He did the same with the back door. When they were seated on the bench, she looked at him.

"Talk to me, Carter."

She listened with astonishment while he explained about

the kidnapping and the painful, fruitless search for Randi that had followed. He told her about his father's untimely heart attack and death, and Carter's and Henri's decision to abandon their search and try to move on with their lives. He told Lily how rotten he'd felt, not knowing his daughter's name, where she was or what she knew about him.

The raw emotion on his face and in his voice made her heart ache, for both him and Henri. Lily owed them each a big apology. "I'm sorry I jumped to the wrong conclusion." Remembering the things she'd said, the dirty looks she'd given him and Henri, she cringed. "What I said—that you're like my father—couldn't be further from the truth. I hope that you'll forgive me…"

"It's not all your fault. I should've told you right away, but the time never seemed right. I've had plenty of time to think about why that was, and the truth is, I was scared. I didn't trust you to understand."

*Carter* didn't trust *her?* Lily hadn't expected this. It stung.

By the tense set of his shoulders, his dark, somber profile as he stared straight ahead instead of at her, Lily knew she'd ruined what could have been a beautiful future together. Her spirits sank. If only she'd been willing to listen sooner…

Now she feared that when he finished, it would be "goodbye and have a nice life."

"I'm sorry you don't trust me," she said. "I wish—"

Carter held up his palm, silencing her. "I'm not through."

Since Lily had said she wanted to listen, that was only fair. She nodded.

"When things between us started to get serious, I figured you had the right to know about my daughter, no matter what. I was on the verge of telling you when she showed up." He gave a rusty laugh. "My timing sucked, huh?"

"I could've been more understanding. You have no idea how terrible I feel."

"Don't," he said. "I'm just glad we finally talked. I've missed you, Lily."

It almost sounded as if he still cared. Daring to hope, she spoke from the heart. "Does this mean you'll give me—and us—a second chance? Because I love you, and I want a future with you."

"You mean that?" For a long moment Carter searched her face. She didn't flinch from his gaze, simply let her love shine through.

"I…" To Lily's shock, his eyes filled with tears. "Oh, hell."

He swiped at them, and her heart swelled to bursting with love and tenderness. Then she was crying, too.

"A fine pair we are." He grinned. "I love you, too, and I'll do whatever it takes to earn your trust."

Lily smiled into his eyes. "You already have it. I never should've doubted you."

"That means everything to me." He pressed his forehead to hers. "I swear that I will never, ever keep anything from you again. Unless it's a surprise."

"I love surprises."

"That's something I didn't know about you. You are the most complex, fascinating woman. I could spend the rest of my life with you and still not know everything about you. But I'd like to try. My house is big enough for all of us—you and me, Hailey and Randi."

"Are you asking us to move in?"

He nodded. "If it's okay with you, I'd like to adopt Hailey with you, and someday help her understand and accept what Janice did."

"You would?" Lily had thought her heart was as full as it

could be. Now it felt even fuller, and she thought she might burst with happiness. "That sounds like a marriage proposal."

"Not very romantic, is it? But then, until a little while ago I didn't think you ever wanted to see me again."

"I think it's the most romantic thing I've ever heard. Yes, Carter Boyle, I'll marry you. It's what I've wanted since the day we met."

Cupping his smiling face between her hands, she drew him down for a kiss. What started out as a tender show of love quickly turned passionate and desperate. When they broke apart, they were both breathing hard.

"Let's go tell Henri and Randi and Hailey the good news," Lily said. "I also want to apologize to your mother."

"I have a better idea," Carter said. "Why don't we stop at the house first, so I can show you just how much I love you?"

"I like the way you think."

He pulled her to her feet. Hand in hand, they walked to his car.

* * * * *

*Celebrate 60 years of pure reading pleasure
with Harlequin®!*
*Silhouette® Romantic Suspense is celebrating with the
glamour-filled, adrenaline-charged series*
LOVE IN 60 SECONDS *starting in April 2009.*
*Six stories that promise to bring the glitz of Las Vegas,
the danger of revenge, the mystery of a missing diamond,
family scandals and ripped-from-the-headlines intrigue.
Get your heart racing as love happens in sixty seconds!*

*Enjoy a sneak peek of*
USA TODAY *bestselling author Marie Ferrarella's*
*THE HEIRESS'S 2-WEEK AFFAIR.*
*Available April 2009
from Silhouette® Romantic Suspense.*

Eight years ago Matt Shaffer had vanished out of Natalie Rothchild's life, leaving behind a one-line note tucked under a pillow that had grown cold: *I'm sorry, but this just isn't going to work.*

That was it. No explanation, no real indication of remorse. The note had been as clinical and compassionless as an eviction notice, which, in effect, it had been, Natalie thought as she navigated through the morning traffic. Matt had written the note to evict her from his life.

She'd spent the next two weeks crying, breaking down without warning as she walked down the street, or as she sat staring at a meal she couldn't bring herself to eat.

Candace, she remembered with a bittersweet pang, had tried to get her to go clubbing in order to get her to forget about Matt.

She'd turned her twin down, but she did get her act together. If Matt didn't think enough of their relationship to try to contact her, to try to make her understand why he'd changed so radically from lover to stranger, then to hell with him. He was dead to her, she resolved. And he'd remained that way.

Until twenty minutes ago.

The adrenaline in her veins kept mounting.

Natalie focused on her driving. Vegas in the daylight wasn't nearly as alluring, as magical and glitzy as it was after dark. Like an aging woman best seen in soft lighting, Vegas's imperfections were all visible in the daylight. Natalie supposed that was why people like her sister didn't like to get up until noon. They lived for the night.

Except that Candace could no longer do that.

The thought brought a fresh, sharp ache with it.

"Damn it, Candy, what a waste," Natalie murmured under her breath.

She pulled up before the Janus casino. One of the three valets currently on duty came to life and made a beeline for her vehicle.

"Welcome to the Janus," the young attendant said cheerfully as he opened her door with a flourish.

"We'll see," she replied solemnly.

As he pulled away with her car, Natalie looked up at the casino's logo. Janus was the Roman god with two faces, one pointed toward the past, the other facing the future. It struck her as rather ironic, given what she was doing here, seeking out someone from her past in order to get answers so that the future could be settled.

The moment she entered the casino, the Vegas phenomena took hold. It was like stepping into a world where time did not matter or even make an appearance. There was only a sense of "now."

Because in Natalie's experience she'd discovered that bartenders knew the inner workings of any establishment they worked for better than anyone else, she made her way to the first bar she saw within the casino.

The bartender in attendance was a gregarious man in his early forties. He had a quick, sexy smile, which was probably one of the main reasons he'd been hired. His name tag identified him as Kevin.

Moving to her end of the bar, Kevin asked, "What'll it be, pretty lady?"

"Information." She saw a dubious look cross his brow. To counter that, she took out her badge. Granted she wasn't here in an official capacity, but Kevin didn't need to know that. "Were you on duty last night?"

Kevin began to wipe the gleaming black surface of the bar. "You mean during the gala?"

"Yes."

The smile gracing his lips was a satisfied one. Last night had obviously been profitable for him, she judged. "I caught an extra shift."

She took out Candace's photograph and carefully placed it on the bar. "Did you happen to see this woman there?"

The bartender glanced at the picture. Mild interest turned to recognition. "You mean Candace Rothchild? Yeah, she was here, loud and brassy as always. But not for long," he added, looking rather disappointed. There was always a circus when Candace was around, Natalie thought. "She and the boss had at it and then he had our head of security escort her out."

She latched on to the first part of his statement. "They argued? About what?"

He shook his head. "Couldn't tell you. Too far away for anything but body language," he confessed.

"And the head of security?" she asked.

"He got her to leave."

She leaned in over the bar. "Tell me about him."

"Don't know much," the bartender admitted. "Just that his name's Matt Shaffer. Boss flew him in from L.A., where he was head of security for Montgomery Enterprises."

There was no avoiding it, she thought darkly. She was going to have to talk to Matt. The thought left her cold. "Do you know where I can find him right now?"

Kevin glanced at his watch. "He should be in his office. On the second floor, toward the rear." He gave her the numbers of the rooms where the monitors that kept watch over the casino guests as they tried their luck against the house were located.

Taking out a twenty, she placed it on the bar. "Thanks for your help."

Kevin slipped the bill into his vest pocket. "Any time, lovely lady," he called after her. "Any time."

She debated going up the stairs, then decided on the elevator. The car that took her up to the second floor was empty. Natalie stepped out of the elevator, looked around to get her bearings and then walked toward the rear of the floor.

"Into the Valley of Death rode the six hundred," she silently recited, digging deep for a line from a poem by Tennyson. Wrapping her hand around a brass handle, she opened one of the glass doors and walked in.

The woman whose desk was closest to the door looked up. "You can't come in here. This is a restricted area."

Natalie already had her ID in her hand and held it up. "I'm looking for Matt Shaffer," she told the woman.

God, even saying his name made her mouth go dry. She was supposed to be over him, to have moved on with her life. What happened?

The woman began to answer her. "He's—"

"Right here."

The deep voice came from behind her. Natalie felt every single nerve ending go on tactical alert at the same moment that all the hairs at the back of her neck stood up. Eight years had passed, but she would have recognized his voice anywhere.

* * * * *

*Why did Matt Shaffer leave heiress-turned-cop*
*Natalie Rothchild?*
*What does he know about the death of*
*Natalie's twin sister?*
*Come and meet these two reunited lovers and learn the*
*secrets of the Rothchild family in*
*THE HEIRESS'S 2-WEEK AFFAIR*
*by USA TODAY bestselling author*
*Marie Ferrarella.*
*The first book in Silhouette® Romantic Suspense's*
*wildly romantic new continuity,*
LOVE IN 60 SECONDS!
*Available April 2009.*

# CELEBRATE
# 60 YEARS
OF PURE READING PLEASURE
## WITH **HARLEQUIN**®!

## Look for Silhouette®
## Romantic Suspense in April!

# *Love In 60 Seconds*
**Bright lights. Big city. Hearts in overdrive.**

Silhouette® Romantic Suspense is celebrating
Harlequin's 60th Anniversary with six stories that
promise to bring readers the glitz of Las Vegas,
the danger of revenge, the mystery of a missing
diamond, and family scandals.

---

**Look for the first title, *The Heiress's 2-Week Affair*
by *USA TODAY* bestselling author
Marie Ferrarella, on sale in April!**

| | |
|---|---|
| *His 7-Day Fiancée* by **Gail Barrett** | May |
| *The 9-Month Bodyguard* by **Cindy Dees** | June |
| *Prince Charming for 1 Night* by **Nina Bruhns** | July |
| *Her 24-Hour Protector* by **Loreth Anne White** | August |
| *5 minutes to Marriage* by **Carla Cassidy** | September |

---

# You're invited to join our Tell Harlequin Reader Panel!

By joining our new reader panel you will:

- Receive Harlequin® books—they are FREE and yours to keep with no obligation to purchase anything!
- Participate in fun online surveys
- Exchange opinions and ideas with women just like you
- Have a say in our new book ideas and help us publish the best in women's fiction

*In addition, you will have a chance to win great prizes and receive special gifts!*
*See Web site for details. Some conditions apply.*
*Space is limited.*

To join, visit us at
## www.TellHarlequin.com.

# REQUEST YOUR FREE BOOKS!
## 2 FREE NOVELS PLUS 2
# FREE GIFTS!

## Love, Home & Happiness!

---

**YES!** Please send me 2 FREE Harlequin® American Romance® novels and my 2 FREE gifts (gifts are worth about $10). After receiving them, if I don't wish to receive any more books, I can return the shipping statement marked "cancel." If I don't cancel, I will receive 4 brand-new novels every month and be billed just $4.24 per book in the U.S. or $4.99 per book in Canada. That's a savings of close to 15% off the cover price! It's quite a bargain! Shipping and handling is just 25¢ per book, along with any applicable taxes.* I understand that accepting the 2 free books and gifts places me under no obligation to buy anything. I can always return a shipment and cancel at any time. Even if I never buy another book from Harlequin, the two free books and gifts are mine to keep forever.

154 HDN EEZK  354 HDN EEZV

Name _____ (PLEASE PRINT)

Address _____ Apt. #

City _____ State/Prov. _____ Zip/Postal Code

Signature (if under 18, a parent or guardian must sign)

### Mail to the **Harlequin Reader Service:**
**IN U.S.A.:** P.O. Box 1867, Buffalo, NY 14240-1867
**IN CANADA:** P.O. Box 609, Fort Erie, Ontario L2A 5X3

Not valid to current subscribers of Harlequin® American Romance® books.

**Want to try two free books from another line?**
**Call 1-800-873-8635 or visit www.morefreebooks.com.**

* Terms and prices subject to change without notice. N.Y. residents add applicable sales tax. Canadian residents will be charged applicable provincial taxes and GST. Offer not valid in Quebec. This offer is limited to one order per household. All orders subject to approval. Credit or debit balances in a customer's account(s) may be offset by any other outstanding balance owed by or to the customer. Please allow 4 to 6 weeks for delivery. Offer available while quantities last.

**Your Privacy:** Harlequin is committed to protecting your privacy. Our Privacy Policy is available online at www.eHarlequin.com or upon request from the Reader Service. From time to time we make our lists of customers available to reputable third parties who may have a product or service of interest to you. If you would prefer we not share your name and address, please check here. ☐

HAR08R2

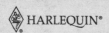

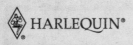

HARLEQUIN®

*American ★ Romance*®

# COMING NEXT MONTH
## Available April 14, 2009

### #1253 A COWBOY'S PROMISE by Marin Thomas
*Men Made in America*

Keeping her Idaho horse farm going has been a struggle for Amy Olsen. Then
ex-rodeo rider Matt Cartwright shows up to collect on a debt. But once he meets
the widow and her two young daughters, Matt's the one who wants to make
good. And when he finds himself falling for Amy, making good is one promise
he intends to keep!

### #1254 FOUND: ONE BABY by Cathy Gillen Thacker
*Made in Texas*

From the moment she comes to the rescue of an abandoned infant on her
neighbor's porch, Michelle Anderson is smitten. But when the sexy doctor next
door, Thad Garner, proposes they join together to adopt the baby, Michelle
refuses to marry without love. So Thad must prove to her that "love, marriage,
baby" can work out—even if you do it in the wrong order!

### #1255 MISTLETOE CINDERELLA by Tanya Michaels
*4 Seasons in Mistletoe*

When Dylan Echols mistakes her for the most popular girl in high school at
their ten-year reunion, Chloe Malcolm seizes the Cinderella moment. The small-
town computer programmer has had a crush on the former big-league pitcher
since forever. But what happens once the clock strikes twelve? Will she turn back
into her tongue-tied former self? Or have a happily-ever-after with the prince of
her dreams?

### #1256 THE GOOD FATHER by Kara Lennox
*Second Sons*

The last thing Max Remington wants is to get involved with Jane Selwyn. Not
only does she work for him, but she's a single mom! It's not that he doesn't like
kids, but they complicate things. And his top priority is building his advertising
agency. Too bad his heart won't listen to his head....

www.eHarlequin.com